William H. Strobridge

Catalogue of the Snow collection of modern silver medals and

coins : with a copious index : in the latter will be found an

interesting variety of American and foreign copper coins and

medals, cut stones, jewelry, and gems : to be sold by auction at t

William H. Strobridge

Catalogue of the Snow collection of modern silver medals and coins : with a copious index : in the latter will be found an interesting variety of American and foreign copper coins and medals, cut stones, jewelry, and gems : to be sold by auction at t

ISBN/EAN: 9783741170881

Manufactured in Europe, USA, Canada, Australia, Japa

Cover: Foto ©Andreas Hilbeck / pixelio.de

Manufactured and distributed by brebook publishing software (www.brebook.com)

William H. Strobridge

Catalogue of the Snow collection of modern silver medals and coins : with a copious index : in the latter will be found an interesting variety of American and foreign copper coins and medals, cut stones, jewelry, and gems : to be sold by auction at t

CATALOGUE

OF THE

SNOW COLLECTION

OF

𝕸odern 𝕾ilber 𝕸edals and 𝕮oins,

WITH A

COPIOUS APPENDIX.

IN THE LATTER WILL BE FOUND AN INTERESTING
VARIETY OF

American and Foreign Copper Coins and Medals,

CUT STONES, JEWELRY, AND GEMS.

><

TO BE SOLD BY AUCTION

AT THE

CLINTON HALL SALE ROOMS,

ASTOR PLACE, NEW YORK,

ON THE AFTERNOONS OF

TUESDAY, WEDNESDAY, AND THURSDAY,

MARCH 19th, 20th, AND 21st,

COMMENCING EACH DAY AT THREE O'CLOCK.

— ><

Messrs. GEO. A. LEAVITT & CO., AUCTIONEERS.

CATALOGUE BY WILLIAM H. STROBRIDGE.

MARCH, 1878.

INDEX.

INTRODUCTION.

ABOUT twenty years ago, Mr. E. J. Snow, of Baltimore, and the writer, who soon after became a resident of that city, commenced life together as amateurs and collectors of *rare old coins ;* we followed our pursuit in great harmony until the breaking out of the war in 1861. Returning to New York in that year, I brought with me all of Mr. Snow's American Coins, leaving with him my own acquisitions, which had been mainly in the early English series.

The great Gilmour collection was then breaking up, and out of it I had obtained many valuable pieces, among them the pattern groat of Edward I., No. 272 of this catalogue, and the Indian Medal of George II., No. 490, of which I have never seen another example. Since that time Mr. Snow has made constant additions to his cabinet, purchasing largely of myself in the earlier years, and directly from Lincoln & Sons, London.

The rare and interesting medal of Henry IV. of France, struck to commemorate the battle of Ivry, was brought to this country by Mr. Barthold, of Baltimore, who died many years ago.

The many beautiful coins and medals of Mexican mint were from the Collection of Brantz Mayer, Esq., who had been a member of the American Legation to Mexico before the war, and author of a valuable work on that country.

Those who have the names of purchasers at the Mickley sale, may see how many valuable coins Mr. Snow derived from that source ; and when I add that Mr. Edward Cogan was for years a caterer for the same Collection, its variety will have been sufficiently suggested.

The number of pieces is not large, but they are generally as fine as possible. They have been catalogued with the most scrupulous care ; my son, who has done most of the work, having referred every doubtful question to gentlemen of experience in the profession.

After a retirement of nearly two years, compelled by what at first threatened to be a total loss of sight, I esteem myself fortunate on my reappearance before my friends, in being able to make my début with this Collection.

W. H. STROBRIDGE.

No. 1 GATES AVE., *February 2d,* 1878.

CATALOGUE.

Coins of Mexico.

["Cob" money conformed to the lawful standard in weight and fineness, but was struck with the hammer without much regard to regularity of form or impression. The "8" which is so conspicuous on the dollars, signifies 8 reals, and, combined with the two columns which always appear rising out of the water on one side of the coins, becomes our dollar mark— thus $.]

1 Cob Dollar, 1752. Long narrow plate dollar, stamped from the dies of the Spanish dollar of 1752. *Kevin*

2 —— Nearly round, stamped over a Spanish dollar. *Har. t.*

3 —— Coin of even thickness, but irregular form. Counter-stamped for Central America. *Hockit.*

4 Cob Half-Dollar. Full weight, cut from a Spanish dollar. Counter-stamped for Central America. *Cogen*

5 Cob Quarter-Dollar. Full weight. Fine. Pierced. *Neal*

6 Cob Eighths of a Dollar. Ordinary. Pierced. 3 pieces

7 A Wedge-shaped Piece cut from a dollar, for circulation when change was scarce. Rare.

8 Set of Cob Money. 1, ½, ¼, ⅛, and ¹⁄₁₆ dollars. The half-dollar counter-stamped for Central America. 5 pieces

9 Dollar of Ferdinand VI., 1760 ; rev. two hemispheres crowned between pillars. VTRAQUE VNUM. *Fine.*

10 Dollar of Ferdinand VII., 1811. Struck for Zacatecas. Rev. a Cross on a mountain top, beneath it L. V. O. MONEDA PROVISIONAL DE ZACATECAS. Fine. Scarce.

11 Plate Dollar, within a circle of scroll-work, at the top, "5 ps.," at the bottom, 1809, across the coin, "FER. VII." ; rev. a crowned shield, surrounded by a similar circle ; in perfect condition and a very rare dollar. Purchased at the Mickley sale for $10.50.

12 Vargas Dollar. 1811. Obv. VARGAS at the top of the coin ; in the center, between two punch marks of pillars, 1811 ; rev. indistinct. This coin was struck with a punch. Very rare.

13 Morelos Silver Dollar. Obv. M 8 R. 1813 ; rev. S U D beneath a bow and arrow. Exceedingly fine. Rare.

ITURBIDE DOLLAR. 1822. Obv. Head facing to right ; rev.
crowned eagle and prickly pear. *M.M* $^{o}_{M}$ (City of Mexico).
Fine proof ; rare.

ITURBIDE DOLLAR. 1824. 1st Republic ; rev. crook-neck
eagle tearing a serpent. Durango mint. Fine. Scarce.

—— Variety. The eagle neck more crooked than in the
ordinary variety. Almost uncirculated ; scarce.

MAXIMILIAN I. 1867. Obv. head to right ; rev. arms, 1
PESO. Only fair.

ITURBIDE DOLLAR, 1867. 2d Republic. Uncirculated and
fine.

HALF-REALS OF ITURBIDE and the Republic. Uncirculated.
Fine.   3 pieces

South and Central America and West Indies.

PERU. Dollar of 1825. Obv. Goddess of Liberty with staff
and shield ; rev. arms of the Republic quartered on a shield,
above, oak wreath and to r. and l. laurel and palm. Uncirculated. Rare.

—— South Peru. Dollar. Cuzco, 1838. Obv. sun and five
stars ; rev. castle and volcano, in background a ship, in foreground a cornucopia. Very fine ; rare.

—— Dollar of 1855. Obv. Goddess of Liberty with spear
and shield ; rev. similar to lot 20. Fair.

—— Un Sol (dollar) of 1864. Obv. figure of Liberty
seated. Uncirculated ; rare.

BOLIVIA. Dollar, 1829. Obv. military bust of Bolivar to right ;
rev. two Llamas lying under a palm-tree ; above, six stars.
Almost uncirculated.

—— Half-dollar. Same type. Uncirculated ; rare.

—— Dollar, 1848. Obv. bare bust of Bolivar to left ; rev.
same. Fine.

—— Dollar of Gen. Melgarejo. Obv. military bust to left.
Al. PACIFICADOR DE BOLIVIA · F. P. ; rev. inscription and date 1865. Fine and rare.

—— Dollar of 1868. New pattern. Obv. LA UNION ES
LA FUERZA, within an oak wreath. I BOLIVIANO
500 G° 9 D° FINO, in exergue, date ; rev. arms. Uncirculated.

CENTRAL AMERICA. Dollar, 1825. Obv. a range of moun-
tain peaks at sunrise. REPUBLICA DEL CENTRO DE
AMERICA and date ; rev. a tree, 8 R., LIBRE CRESCA
FECUNDO, below, mint mark and quality of the silver.
Almost uncirculated.

30 HAYTI. BOYER, PRESIDENT. Dollar, half, quarter, and si
teenth. Fine ; the quarter uncirculated. 4 piec

31 ——— Petron, President. Quarter and eighth of a dollar. Fin
4 piec

32 ——— Obv. 25 * C and 12 * C within a ring formed by a se
pent ; rev. martial implements and tree surmounted by
Liberty Cap. Uncirculated. 5 piec

33 PROCLAMATION MEDALLETS of Ferdinand VII. struck fc
Guatemala. Obv. bust ; rev. arms crowned "Inter suspiri
Fides" and one of the Republic ; obv. arms surmounte
by the top of a quiver ; rev. inscription. Uncirculated ; tw
proofs. Rare. Size, 13. 3 piec

34 ——— Obv. bust ; rev. QUE SALTENANGO and GRANL
ENG. SANTA ANA. Fine ; rare. Size, 13. 3 piec

34 GUATEMALA. Obv. "Inicio Por Jurados," etc. ; rev. "F
Pueblo Juez." Proof. Size, 1

Spain and Portugal.

35 PHILIP II. 1583. Quarter dollar. Military bust to r. ; rev
arms and inscription. Fair ; rare.

36 CHARLES II. DOLLAR of 1673, struck for Brabant. Arms or
both sides. Called *Duro* 8 Reals. Extremely fine ; scarce.

37 CHARLES IV. Dollar of 1804. Obv. laureated head ; rev.
shield beneath a crown bearing a crowned lion, a castle and
fleur-de-lis. *Splendid proof.*

38 JOSEPH NAPOLEON. Dollar of twenty Reals, 1809. Fair ; rare.

39 FERDINAND VII. Dollar of 1821. Almost uncirculated.

40 AMADEUS I. 1871. Obv. bust, bare ; rev. arms, 5 PESETAS.
Fine ; rare.

41 JOHN VI. (Portugal). 1818. 960 Reis. Cross covered by a
globe, with arms of Portugal. Struck over a Spanish dollar.
Uncirculated.

Coins of France.

42 CHARLES III., 895. Penny. Rare. Mickley sale, lot 892.

43 PHILIP II., Duke of Guise, 1108. Penny. Rare. Mickley,
897.

44 RAIMUNDUS IV., Count of Toulouse, 1224. Penny. Obv. J. ;
rev. cross in circle. *Very fine.* Rare. Mickley, 905.

45 ——— Another. Obv. star and crescent ; rev. double cross.
As fine as when struck. Cost 8 shillings.

Silver Cabinet.

LOUIS IX. 1270. Groat. Very rare. Mickley, 908.

PHILIP IV. 1310. Penny. Fine; rare. " 911.

PHILIP V. (The Fine), 1321. Groat. Very rare. Mickley, 914.

CHARLES IV. (The Fine), 1322. Groat. Very fine; rare. Mickley, 916.

PHILIP (The Good), 1361, Duke of Burgundy. Groat. Fine; rare. Mickley, 920.

JOHN I., 1364, Duke of Burgundy. Obv. shield; rev. cross, with fleur-de-lis in the angles. Fine; rare. Mickley, 921.

JOHN, COUNT OF ANGOULÊME. 1376. Penny. Very fine. Rare. Mickley, 927.

CHARLES VI. 1380. Groat. Fine; rare.

LEWIS, COUNT OF MALL, 1383. Said to be the last Count of Flanders. Fine Groat. Mickley, 935.

CHARLES VII. 1422. Penny. Rare.

—— Groat. Very fine; rare.

—— Another. Fine; rare.

CHARLES VIII. (The Affable). 1483. Grand-blanc. Obv. large R. crowned; rev. cross, ordinary. Rare.

—— Groat. Fine; rare.

—— Broad groat. Very fine; rare.

FRANCIS I. 1515. Penny. F crowned under crown; rev. cross. Fine; very rare.

HENRY II. 1547. Groat. H crowned, 3 fleur-de-lis; rev. a cross and 3 fleur-de-lis. Very fine and rare. Mickley, 960.

HENRY III. 1574. Groat. Similar to last. H and crown smaller. Fine; very rare.

HENRY IV. 1589. Gros Tournois.

CHARLES IX. (son of Henry II.) Shilling. 1560. Shilling of fine silver; obv. CAROLUS VIII. D. G. FRANC. REX, laureated bust of the king. 1560 ; rev. SIT NOMEN DNI BENEDIC MDLXII. Arms of France under a large crown, C crowned on each side. Fine.

HENRY III. 1574. Half-crown. Obv. laureated bust. HERI CUS III. D. G. FRANC. ET POL. REX. 1581. 1581 rev. cross fleurie; H in center SIT NOMEN, etc. Fine very rare.

—— Shilling. C under bust. Poor

HENRY II. (Henry IV. of France) of Navarre, 1583. Obv. draped bust, head laureated, 1581 an ox. HENRICUS II. D. G. REX NAVARRE D.; rev. cross formed of crowned Hs, and crossing it a cross-fleurie GRATIA DEI SUM ID QVOD SVM. Very rare.

From the beginning of the 16th century until the elevation of Henry the Fourth to the throne of France the kingdom of Navarre was but a petty State, comprised of the villages of Saint Jean, Pied-de-Port, Saint Palais and Grammont.—ROBERT, page 101.

69 LOUIS XIII. (The Just). 1610. Crown. Almost uncirculated; *splendid.*

70 LOUIS XIV. (Le Grande Monarch). 1643. Crown 1651. Young head. Equal to last.

71 —— Crown 1690. Middle-aged head; rev. cross formed by eight crowned Ls, a fleur-de-lis in each angle, CHRS REGN VINC IMP. *MM* M. (Toulouse). Very fine ; rare.

72 —— Crown, 1713. Old head ; rev. three crowns and three fleur-de-lis. SIT NOMEN, etc., *MM* E (Tours). Almost uncirculated.

73 —— Half-crown, 1651. Young head. As fine as the crown.

74 —— Half-crown, 1690. *MM* H (La Rochelle). Sharp and fine ; uncirculated ; showing very slightly its contact with the velvet of the cabinet.

75 —— Half-crown. Old head, 1712. *MM* A (Paris). A match for the crown.

76 LOUIS XV. 1715. Crown, 1759. Young head. Obv. filleted head, Pelican (?) beneath ; rev. arms in an oval beneath a crown enclosed within two branches ; SIT NOMEN, etc. Almost uncirculated ; very fine. *MM* A (Paris).

77 —— Crown, 1774. Old head, pomegranate beneath. *MM* cow (Pau). Very fine.

78 LOUIS XVI. 1774. Crown, 1783. Uncirculated ; the reverse *splendid* ; *MM* a cow.

79 —— Crown. 1793. Rev. History writing the Constitution on a tablet ; fasces surmounted by a liberty cap to l. ; a cock to r. REGNE DE LA LOI.; in exergue, L'AN 5 DE LA LIBERTE. *MM* M (Toulouse). Very fine.

This coin was struck the first year of the Republic. The obv. still retaining the head of the king with his title.

80 —— Another. Slightly different from last. Beneath the head a lion ; on the rev., to left of the fasces, a lyre. *MM* A (Paris). If anything, better than last.

81 —— Half-crown. Same type and condition as last.

The above 13 lots are the finest series of Louis XIII., XIV., XV. and XVI. that have been offered for sale in this country for many a year. Mr. Snow took great pains in selecting them, and spared no expense. Most of them he imported. In this condition they are rare.

82 EIGHTH OF A CROWN of Louis XIV., and one of Louis XIV. Uncirculated. 2 pieces

83 SIXTEENTH OF A CROWN of Louis XIII., and one of Louis XIV. Fine. 2 pieces

84 NAPOLEON BONAPARTE. An. 12. Premier Consol, 5 francs by *Tiolier*. Better than fair ; rare.

85 NAPOLEON, EMPEROR. 1804. Five Francs, 1813, by *Tiolier*. *MM* cock. Uncirculated and brilliant ; rare.

Silver Cabinet.

LOUIS XVIII, 1815. Five Francs, 1814; by *Tiolier*; rev. arms; PIÈCE DE 5 FRANCS. Uncirculated; rare.

LOUIS PHILIPPE I. Five Francs. By *Tiolier*. Fine; especially the rev.

REPUBLIC OF 1848. Five Francs by Dupré. 1848. Obv. three figures standing, LIBERTÉ, ÉGALITÉ, FRATERNITÉ; rev. REPUBLIC FRANCAIS 5 FRANCS. Uncirculated and brilliant.

—— Five Francs of 1850, by *E. A. Oudiné*. Obv. head of Ceres; rev. like those of '48. Equal to last.

LOUIS NAPOLEON BONAPARTE as Pres. of the Republic. 1852. By *Barre*. Obv. bare bust; rev. REPUBLIQUE FRANCAISE 5 FRANCS. Brilliant proof; rare.

NAPOLEON III. 1852. Five Francs. By *Barre*. Obv. bare bust. NAPOLEON EMPEREUR; rev. crown crowned, displaying two sceptres crossed, with the eagle of the Empire. Five Francs, 1854. Proof; scarce.

REPUBLIC OF 1871. Five Francs. *Dupré*. LIBERTÉ, ÉGALITÉ, FRATERNITÉ, 1873. Proof. *HM* anchor and bee.

QUART OF NAPOLEON I. One-fourth Franc of Louis Philippe; and 10-cent of Napoleon III. Fine. 3 pieces

---

Fine Crowns.
(*Arranged according to dates.*)

SILVESTRE VALERIO, DOGE OF VENICE. Obv. Saint holding a cross blessing the Doge, who is kneeling. DVX SILV VALERIO S M VENET in ex. FT; rev. Lion of St. Mark, standing on his hind legs, carrying cross and palm-branch, PUES ET VICTORIA. Very rare and rare.

Size, 17

JOHN HUSS. Obv. bust in cap, IOA-HVS CREDO VNAM ESSE ECCLESIAM SANCTAM CATOLICAN; rev. Huss bound to the stake, within a circle. ANNO, A CHRIST NATO 1415 IO HVS CENTVM REVOLVTIS ANNIS DEO RESPONDEBITIS ET MIHI. Fine and rare old crown. Size, 26

MAURICE, DUKE OF SAXONY, **1543.** Obv. bust in armor; rev. bust of John, with drawn sword. Very fine and rare.

JAMES VI. SWORD DOLLAR OF 1571. Issued by authority of the Lord Regent. Obv. arms of Scotland crowned, IACOBVS 6 DEI GRATIA REX SCOTORVM I and R crowned to r. and L. of shield; rev. a crown on the point of a sword. XXX PRO ME SI MEREOR IN ME. Countermarked with a thistle. Almost uncirculated, and in this condition very rare.

Fine Crowns.

99 HENRY JULIUS, DUKE OF BRUN AND LUNEBURG. Obv. w
man carrying a double-headed arrow in one hand and tor
in the other; at his feet a dog, 15–95, in the field, D.C.S.C
rev. within a circle, surrounded by eleven shields, a group
figures in the act of prayer; above them, N.R.M.AD.I.P
written on the clouds. Very fine and rare crown. Size,

100 JOHN CASIMIR AND JOHN EARNEST. 1598. Obv. their bu
face to face; rev. coat of arms surrounded by thirte
shields. Fine half-crown.

101 MAXIMILIAN, ARCH-DUKE OF AUSTRIA. 1603. Obv. figu
of the duke in armor, standing; rev. knight on horsebac
armed cap-a-pie riding to left, within a circle of fifteen shield
Splendid uncirculated crown; rare. Size,

102 CHRISTIAN II., DUKE OF SAXONY. Obv. bust in armor, wi
drawn sword. 16–06. Rev. busts of John George a
Augustus. Fine old crown. Size,

103 FRANCIS ERIZZO, DOGE OF VENICE. Obv. winged bust of
lion on a shield. SANCTVS MARCVS VENET; in exergu
"140."; rev. ornate cross, FRANC. ERIZZO DVX VE
D. R. Beautiful and rare crown; barely circulated. Ve
rare. Size,

104 HENRY JULIUS, DUKE OF BRUNS. AND LUN. 1612. Ol
wild man carrying an uprooted pine-tree in his hand; re
coat of arms surmounted by five crests. Fine. Size,

105 PHILIP ERNEST, COUNT OF MANSFIELD. 1619. Obv. tl
duke on horseback, slaying the dragon; rev. coat of an
and two crests. Fine broad crown; rare. Size,

106 PETER ERNEST, DUKE OF MANSFIELD. Same type as la
Very good crown; rare. Size,

107 ROBT. HUGO AND JOHN, COMITES IN MONTFOR
Shield and helmet surmounted by a bishop's mitre; re
double-headed eagle. FERDINANDVS II IX G. RO]
IMP. S.A. 1622. Uncirculated crown; very rare. Size,

108 JOHN GEORGE, DUKE OF SAXONY. Obv. bust to the wai
with drawn sword; rev. coat of arms with six crests, 16–2
Fine old crown. Size,

109 ROME. URBAN VIII. 1623. Bust in rich robes and regali
below, AN. XII. rev. St. Michael slaying the dragon—tl
combat in the air. Well preserved and rare scudo. Size,

110 ROME. SAINT EMBASSIES. Obv. seated figure of the sai
with mitre and crosier; rev. double-headed eagle. Stru
under Ferdinand II. Very fine old crown. Size,

111 TEUTONIC ORDER. JOHN EUSTACHIUS, G. M. Uncirculat
and beautiful crown of 1625. Order, arms, titles, etc.; re
St. Mary standing with infant Jesus. ORD. INTE. Supe
crown; well marked RR. Size,

112 VENICE. ODOARDUS FARNESE. Doge, 1626. Obv. his bus
rev. St. Vitalis holding sceptre. "SCVDO in ex. Fi
old crown; very rare. Size,

12   *Silver Cabinet.*

113 FERDINAND II. Crown of 1637. Obv. full-length figure of
the emperor in armor, with sword, sceptre, and mund; rev.
double-headed eagle. Obv. very fine.

114 GEORGE HERTZOG, BRUNS. AND LUNE. 1641. Obv. wild
man carrying an uprooted tree ; rev. coat of arms surmounted by four crests. Fine and rare crown.

115 CHRISTIAN FREDERICK, DUKE OF MANSFIELD. Crown of
1653. Obv. the duke on horseback to l., slaying the
dragon ; rev. arms, surmounted by a helmet supporting
seven flags. INMANS PELT, etc. Very fine and rare.

116 CHARLES LOUIS, OF BAVARIA. Crown of 1659. Obv. bust to
the waist in armor; rev. three shields surmounted by a helmet bearing a crowned lion. DOMINVS PROVIDEBIT.
Fine.

117 LEOPOLD L. OF AUSTRIA. Half-crown of 1639. Laureated
head. Fine.

118 CHARLES V. Crown of 1659. Obv. full-length figure of the
emperor, with sceptre and mund. CARLVS QVINT; rev.
double-headed eagle. MONETA CIVIT BISVNTINE.
Almost uncirculated, and in this condition very rare.

119 ANTON GUNTHER. Broad crown of 1660. Bust three-quarter
face to r.; rev. arms crowned. AVX ILLVM MEAM A
DOMINO. On each side of the arms a flower (48 GROT).
Very fine and rare.   Size, 28

120 ROME. ALEXANDER VII. Obv. St. Peter supporting arms of
the Popes; rev. man giving alms to a pauper with a wooden
leg. Scudo in good preservation, and very rare.   Size, 27

121 MAX. HENRY (Bavaria). Archbishop of Cologne. Crown of
1671. Obv. bust, head bare ; rev. arms crowned. Fine;
rare.

122 MAGDEBURG. Two-third Crown of 1674. Obv. Margaret at
the city gate ; rev. inscription. Fine and rare.

123 I. ANONHRS. Two-third Crown. Obv. helmet surmounted
by a peacock with tail spread ; rev. Moneta, etc., 1675.
Uncirculated; rare.
I have never met with another piece of this description.—W. H. S.

124 EXDURIS GLORIA. Dollar (⅔). John Frederick, Duke
Brun. and Lune. 1687. Fine ; rare.

125 RUDOLPH AUGUSTUS AND ANTHONY ULRICH, DUKES OF BRUN.
AND LUNE. Broad Crown of 1691. Obv. two wild men;
rev. arms surmounted by five crests. Very fine ; rare.
                                                      Size, 29

126 HOHENLOHE. WOLFGANG JULIUS, PRINCE OF NEUENSTEIN.
Splendid uncirculated crown of 1697. Bust in armor with
shield; rev. cavalier galloping over prostrate figures. Rare.
                                                      Size, 27

127 ANTHONY ULRICH. Broad Crown of 1704. Wild man stripping branches from a tree. Superb coin ; rare.   Size, 26

128 LUCCA. **Crown of 1747.** St. Martin on horseback, giving half his cloak to a beggar; rev. arms, Lucenses Respublica. Uncirculated; rare. *Size, 27*

129 —— Another, 1753. Obv. same; rev. two lions supporting arms. *Almost* uncirculated; rare. *Size, 24*

130 POLAND. FRED. AUGUSTUS. Crown of 1763. Bust richly draped; rev. arms on two shields, one with twenty-five divisions, the other with four. *Fine; rare.*

131 PETER, DUKE OF SEMIGALLIA. Fine, broad Crown of 1780. Rare. *Size, 27*

131* STRASBURG. Crown. Lions with fleur-de-lis supporting arms of the city; rev. a lily. *Very fine* and rare.

132 —— Another. Different motto. Equally fine and rare.

133 BELGIUM. Crown. Arms; rev. figure representing Liberty. HANC TVEMVR. HAC NITIMVR. Uncirculated.

134 SICILY. FERDINAND IV. AND CAROLINE. Crown. 1791. Their busts jugata; rev. SOLI REDUCI. A blazing sun and section of the zodiac; a globe below. *Extremely fine; rare.*

135 MALTA. DOLLAR OF ROHAN. 1796. F. EMANUEL DE ROHAN. M.M. Uncirculated; rare.

136 FULDA. ADALBERTUS, BISHOP OF. Convention Crown of 1796. Obv. bust; rev. coat of arms crowned. PRO DEO ET PATRIA. Uncirculated; nearly proof impression.

137 FREDERICK WILLIAM III. OF PRUSSIA. 1799. Military bust to l. "F. W. III. Rex Bor. Pr. Sup. Novici & Val;" rev. arms supported by two wild men. "Suum Cuique," in ex. "1 1/2 HZ." Struck for Switzerland. Proof; very rare. *Size, 22*

138 BAMBERG. CHRISTOPHER FRANCIS BISHOP. Convention Crown. 1800. Shield bearing arms on a crowned ermine; rev. view of the city. ACH DEM CONVENTION SEUSE. Uncirculated.

139 FRANCIS HERTZOG, OF SAXONY. Beautiful proof Dollar of 1805.

140 CHARLES LOUIS AND M. ALOYSIA, of Tuscany. Beautiful Dollar (double thaler) of 1807. Their busts jugata; rev. arms. Rare. *Size, 28*

141 —— 1804. Dollar (thaler). Equally fine; rare.

142 NAPLES. Dollar of Joachim Murat. Head to left, hair curly; rev. Dodeci Carlini (12 Carlini). Fine; very rare.

143 —— Obv. figure of Liberty, standing; rev. CARLINA SEI (six Carlini). Uncirculated; very rare.

144 LUCCA. FELIX AND ELISA. Their heads conjoined; rev. 5 FRANCHI. 1807. Uncirculated.

145 FREDERICK, PRINCE OF WALDECK. Beautiful proof Crown of 1810. Rare and valuable.

146 JEROME NAPOLEON, KING OF WESTPHALIA. Two-third Crown
of 1811. Laureated head to r. Fine.

147 FERDINAND VII., KING OF SPAIN. Dollar of 1820. Laureated
head to r. ; rev. arms between two pillars. Fair.

148 MEXICAN DOLLAR OF ITURBIDE. 1822. Very fine.

149 DOLLAR OF PERU. 1852. Fine impression, uncirculated.

150 LOUIS I., KING OF BAVARIA. Obv. bare head to r. ; rev. monument of the Son of King Otto. 1834. Fine dollar.

151 ——— Rev. view of a church. 1836. Fine proof.

152 5 LIRE OF VENICE. Obv. lion. 22 March, 1848. Uncirculated.

153 PIUS IX. Obv. bust to left ; rev. Scudo 1835, within a beautiful wreath. Proof.

154 WILLIAM, KING OF WÜRTEMBURG. Obv. bust ; rev. lion and stag supporting a shield. 1846. ZWEY GULDEN. Uncirculated and beautiful coin.

155 THALER OF FRANKFURT. 1856. Obv. eagle ; rev. "Ein Gedenkthaler." Uncirculated.

156 FRANCIS II., KING OF SICILY. Uncirculated Dollar of 1859. Obv. bare head to l. ; rev. arms, G. 120.

157 FREE STATE OF FRANKFORT. Double Dollar of 1861. Obv. female head to r. crowned with oak leaves. Uncirculated and brilliant.

158 GEORGE, KING OF HANOVER. Double Dollar of 1862. Obv. bare bust to l. ; rev. lion and unicorn upholding shield bearing the arms of Great Britain and Hanover. Uncirculated and brilliant.

159 FREDERICK FRANCIS, KING OF WÜRTEMBURG. Thaler of 1867. Uncirculated.

160 HALF-PAGODA of Hindostan.   Size, 23

Austria and Hungary.

161 SIGISMUND (Tyrol). 1439 to 1296. Crown. Full-length figure of the Emperor ; rev. a Knight armed cap-a-pie galloping to right. 1486 below ; around, circle of sixteen shields. Extremely fine ; rare.

162 FERDINAND I. 1564. Crown without date. Bust of the Emperor to the hips in mail, with sceptre and sword ; rev. coat of arms. Fine ; rare.   Size, 26

163 ——— Thick crown. Similar to last, but from a different die. Very fine ; rare.

164 MAXIMILIAN. 1590. Crown. Obv. the Emperor standing in armour with a sword in his hand ; rev. a Knight on horseback armed galloping to right ; beneath horse 1603 ; around, a circle of fifteen shields. Very fine ; rare.

165 Maximilian. Crown, 1615. Obv. draped bust, with high ruff; rev. coat of arms. Uncirculated, brilliant, a superb coin; rare.

166 Rudolph II. 1600. Crown. Obv. bust in armor, with high collar, head laureated; rev. coat of Arms. Very fine; rare; two slight scratches on planchet in front of the face.

167 Albert and Elisabeth. 1619. Crown. Their busts jugate; rev. arms upheld by lions, above them a crown. Better than fair; rare.

168 Ferdinand II. 1619 to 1637. Crown, 1623. Obv. full-length figure of the Emperor in armor, with sceptre and mund; rev. double-headed eagle and lion of Bohemia.

169 —— Broad crown, 1631. Obv. draped bust, with high ruff, head laureated; rev. double-headed eagle, crowned, bearing a crowned shield and carrying a sword in each talon. Nobly uncirculated; very fine. Size 29

170 —— Crown struck for Vienna, 1626. Obv. crowned eagle carrying in one talon a sword and sceptre; in the other the mund; rev. ornate shield bearing a pineapple. AVGVSTA VIN DELICORVM, 1626. Better than fair.

171 Ferdinand III. 1637 to 1657. Crown. Obv. bust richly draped, head laureated; rev. double-headed eagle bearing a shield crowned, carrying a sword and sceptre. Fine.

172 —— Crown of 1641. Obv. bust in armor, head laureated; rev. view of the city of Wien, in the foreground a pineapple. Uncirculated.

173 Leopold. 1625 to 1632. Double crown of 1626. Obv. bust to the waist in armor, carrying sword and sceptre, head crowned; rev. single-headed eagle, crowned. Uncirculated; rare.

174 —— Crown of 1632. Obv. same as last; rev. shield with coat of arms beneath a crown, surrounded by a royal order. Uncirculated.

175 Leopold I. (Surnamed the "Hog-mouth"). 1658 to 1705. Crown. Obv. bust in armor, head laureated; rev. coat of arms. 1662. Fine.

176 —— Crown of 1685. Obv. bust in armor, head laureated and hair in long curls; rev. coat of arms. Uncirculated.

177 —— Half-crown, 1695. Obv. same as preceding; rev. double-headed eagle. Uncirculated.

178 Charles VI. 1711 to 1740. Crown of 1737. Obv. bust in armor, head laureated; rev. double-headed eagle. Uncirculated; splendid crown.

178 Maria Theresa. 1740 to 1780. Crown of 1780. Proof.

178* Francis I. (New dynasty). 1804 to 1830. Proof crown of 1830, struck for Hungary; rev. Virgin and Child.

179 Ladislaus (Hungary). Crown of 1506. Obv. the King on horseback within an ornamental circle; SANCTVS LADIS-LAVS REX VNGARIE; rev. coat of arms. Very fine and valuable old crown; rare.

180 GABRIEL BETHLEN (Hungary). 1620 to 1628. Crown of 1621. Bust to the waist in armor, head bare; rev. coat of arms, TRANS. PRINCEPS. ET. SICVLOR. COM. broad and fine coin, nearly uncirculated; rare.

181 GEORGE RAKOVI. II. 1649 to 1660. Crown. Obv. bust to the waist in armor, carrying sceptre, cap and aigrette of feathers, GEORGIVS RAKO. D. G. P. T.; rev. coat of arms and crown, PAR. REG. HVN. DOM. ET. SIC. COM. 1658. Sharp and fine ; rare.

Brunswick and Luneburg.

182 CHRISTIANUS. 1631. Crown. Obv. bust in armor, with two royal orders ; rev. coat of arms with five crests. Very fine and rare. Size, 27

183 AVGVSTVS. 1636. First Bell Dollar (Glockenthaler) Obv. figure of the Duke to the knee in armor; rev. ALLES MIT BEDACHT. ANNO 1635. Bell, T.S.G.E.B., UT. SIC. NISI. Very fine ; rare.

184 —— Fourth Bell Dollar. Inscription on obv. and rev. same as last. Instead of the bell is a clapper lying on a box, 13 K. MAH on the clapper and AP. V. 13. to IN. F on the box. SEDT beneath. Very fine ; rare.

185 FREDERICK HERTZOG. 1642. Crown. Obv. bust in armor, with deep lace collar; rev. coat of arms with five crests. Very fine ; rare. Size, 27

186 CHRISTIAN LVDOVICVS (Duke). 1653. Crown. Obv. horse galloping within a circle of olive branches, SINCERE ET CONSTANTER ; rev. coat of arms with five crests, CHRISTIAN LVDOVICVS. D. G. DVX. BR. ET LVNEBVRG. Fine ; rare. Size, 28

187 AGESTVS HERTZZOG. 1656. Crown. Obv. wild man carrying an uprooted pine tree field horizontally, ALLES MIT BEDACHT. ; rev. coat of arms with five crests. Extremely fine ; rare. Size, 28

188 JOHN FREDERICK (Duke). 1674. Twenty-four M. Groschen (Two-third Crown). Obv. wild man carrying a pine tree ; rev. EX DVRIS GLORIA. Very fine and rare.

189 —— 1676. Two-third Crown. Obv. draped bust, hair in long curls ; rev. palm tree growing out of a rock in the water, ships in offing, EX DVRIS GLORIA. Nearly uncirculated ; rare.

190 —— 1679. Broad Crown. Obv. draped bust in armor, the hair in curls descending to his shoulders ; rev. palm tree growing out of a pile of rocks, EX DVRIS GLORIA. Uncirculated and superb coin ; rare. Size, 30

191 ANTHONY ULRICH. 1694. Two-third Crown. Obv. wild man stripping a tree of its branches; rev. REMIGIO ALTISSIMI UNI, 1694. Very fine.

192 —— Broad Crown. 1714. Obv. wild man, CONSTANTER; rev. coat of arms with five crests. Very fine; rare. Size, 29.

193 GEORGE LUDWIG (made King of England in 1714 as George I.) 1705. Two-third Crown. Obv. wild man, IN RECTU DECUS. Uncirculated.

194 AUGUSTUS WILHELM. 1718. Broad Crown. Obv. wild man, PARTATVERI; rev. coat of arms with five crests. Very fine. Size, 30

195 GEORGE I. (England). Broad crown. Arms on four shields arranged in the form of a cross; rev. wild man. Better than fair; rare. Size, 30

196 GEORGE II. Crown. 1743. Arms on shield under a crown; rev. St. Andrew. Milled rim, fair; rare. Size, 26

197 GEORGE III. 1805. Two-third Crown. Obv. arms on a square shield. Very fine.

198 GEORGE IV. 1825. Two-third Crown. Obv. filleted head to left. Equally fine.

199 WILLIAM IV. 1833. Another. Obv. arms on circular shield beneath a crown. Proof.

————

Saxony.

200 KLAPPMUTZEN THALER. (The oldest Saxon Crown). Busts of Frederick, with John and George, all wearing caps; Frederick on obv. with drawn sword; the others *viz a viz* on the rev. From 1486 to 1525. Very fine and rare.

201 MAURICE. 1544. Crown. Obv. bust of the Duke; rev. bust of John with drawn sword. Fine old Crown. Rare.

202 AUGUSTUS. 1553 to 1586. Crown of 1573. Obv. bust in armor with drawn sword; rev. coat of arms with three crests. Fine.

203 JOHN CASIMIR and John Earnest. Crown of 1615. Their busts face to face; rev. a Knight on horseback within a circle surrounded by sixteen shields. Almost uncirculated.

204 —— Half-crown, 1590. Same obv.; rev. coat of arms in a circle, surrounded by twelve shields. Fine.

205 FREDERICK, WILLIAM, AND JOHN. 1593. Half-crown. Their busts to the waist; rev. coat of arms surmounted by three crests. Fair; rare.

206 CHRISTIAN II. Bust of Christian between John George and Augustus, 1595; rev. same as preceding. Fine broad crown.

207 —— 1603. Obv. bust to the waist in armor, holding a drawn sword; rev. busts of John George and Augustus in a circle, surrounded by fourteen shields. *Fine.*

208 JOHN GEORGE. Crown, 1616. Obv. King on horseback, with drawn sword, PRO LEGE ET REGE; coat of arms under the horse; rev. inscription in twelve lines. Fine and rare old crown. Size 27

209 —— Crown of 1612. Obv. bust of the Duke in armor, with a sword in one hand, and a helmet in the other ; rev. bust of Augustus within a double circle, surrounded by eighteen shields. Very fine and rare.

210 —— Crown of 1653. Obv. similar ; rev. coat of arms with eight crests. *Very fine.*

211 DOLLAR, OR EIGHT DUCAT. 8 FRA. DVC SAXON. Four busts on each side. Has been gilt. Fair ; scarce.

212 DOLLAR WITH THE BUSTS of four brothers, Dukes of Saxony, 1615. Their busts to the hips in full regalia; heads bare. IO PHIL, FR. IO WIL. FA ER. WIL. Very fine.

213 JOHN PHILIP. Crown, 1623. Obv. bust in armor, to the waist, head bare ; rev. busts of his three brothers in armor. Equally fine.

214 FREDERICK CHRISTIAN. 1763. Two-third Crown. Obv. bust ; rev. coat of arms. Fine.

215 FREDERICK AUGUSTUS. 1790. One-third Crown. Obv. bare bust to it ; rev. double-headed eagle. Proof.

216 ANTON AND FREDERICK AUGUSTUS. King and Regent. Crown, 1831. Obv. their busts jugata ; rev. scroll. Uncirculated.

217 FREDERICK AUGUSTUS II. 1854. Thaler. Obv. bare bust ; rev. shield with the arms of Saxony between two seated females, with attributes of justice and hope. Uncirculated.

Switzerland.

218 HELVETIAN REPUBLIC. 1798. 40 BATZEN. Fine Crown. Nearly proof.

219 —— 1861. Obv. William Tell ; rev. 4 Franken. Fine proof dollar.

220 CANTON ZURICH. 1818. 40 BATZEN. Obv. arms; rev. DOMINE CONSERVA NOS IN PACE. Splendid proof dollar.

221 CANTON BERNE. 1835. Obv. shield in a sunk oval, bearing the arms of the Canton (a Bear) crowned. RESPUBLICA BERNENSIS; rev. DOMINUS PROVIDE BIT. Tell standing in a sunken oval, in ex. 1835. Splendid proof dollar.

222 CANTON GRAUBÜNDEN, 4 SCHWEITER FRANKEN ; three shields beneath, three clasped hands emerging from the clouds ; rev. shield and trophy of arms. 1842. Fine proof.

223 CANTON GENEVA. Obv. arms. POST TENEBRAS LUX; rev. REPUBLIQUEET CANTON DE GENEVE; within a wreath of oak and laurel, 10 FRANCS. 1848. By *Borg.* Splendid proof.

224 HELVETIA, under the Constitution of 1848. 5 francs. The Canton personified as a woman seated leaning on a shield. Very fine.

225 ——— Obv. female seated, in ex. 5 FRANCS; rev. shield under a cross with two guns and two flags crossed, behind TIR FEDERAL A LACHAUX-DE-FONDS, JUILLET 1863. Splendid proof. Rare.

Sweden.

226 CAROLUS IX. 1608. Obv. full-length figure of the King in armor, holding a sword in one hand, and a globe in the other; rev. Saviour standing, SALVATOR MUNDI SALVANOS. Fine crown. Rare. Mickley, 1420.

227 CHRISTINA. 1643. Obv. bust of the Queen richly dressed. Head crowned and ¾ face. The hair is long and descends to the shoulders. CHRISTINA. D. G. SVE. GOT. WAN. Q. DE REG ET PR. HÆ.; rev. Saviour standing holding a globe. SALVATOR MUNDI SALVA NOS. MDCXLIII. Almost uncirculated crown. Mickley, 1423.

228 CAROLUS X. Half-dollar. Obv. laureated head; rev. 3 crowns. 1664. IIM. Fair.

229 ULRICA ELINORA. Obv. bust. ULRICA ELINORA DG. REGINA. SVEC; rev. arms quartered on a shield crowned, two lions supporting. Gud Mitt hopp. 1719. Nearly uncirculated crown. Mickley, 1435.

230 FREDERICUS. Obv. bust in armor, draped, head bare; hair long and curled. FREDERICUS D.G. REX. SVECIE; rev. arms on a crowned shield, supported by two lions. Gud Mitt hopp. *Very fine* crown.

231 GUSTAVUS III. Obv. bare bust; rev. arms of Sweden, surrounded by a royal collar and crown, I R⁹. 1779. Almost uncirculated.

232 CHARLES XIV. Splendid uncirculated dollar. Obv. bare bust, curly hair; rev. arms, lion on a square escutcheon. SP⁵. 1824.

Denmark.

233 CHRISTIAN IV. Obv. the King at full length, walking with sword and sceptre; rev. large crown in a circle, 1620 R. F. P. and inscription. Splendid crown; rare.

234 FREDERICK III. 1659 (crown). IIII. Marck Danske. Obv. I and 3 housed, beneath crown EBENEZER.; rev. an arm reaching out of a cloud, beneath a crown, severing a hand from an arm. This represents Holland delivering Denmark from Sweden. Fine and rare.

235 ———— II. Marck Danske. (Half **crown**) 1665. Obv. monogram; rev. crowned **lion** holding an axe. **Fine.**

236 CHRISTIAN VII. Specie daler for **Holstein, 1793**; obv. bust.; rev. arms. Scarce.

237 FREDERICK IV. Four marks (crown), 1703. Obv. king on horseback, pointing forward with a sceptre; rev. arms. **Fair; rare.**

238 **FREDERICK VII.** Mortuary dollar, 1848. Obv. head of the **king; rev.** head of Christian VIII. Fine. **Rare.**

Siege Pieces, etc.

239 OXFORD. **Charles I., England.** Obv. **C.R.** under a crown rev. large $\underset{\text{V}}{\text{s}}$ (five shillings). As good as the piece is usually found. Rare.

240 SARMATIA. Square dollar of Wolfgang Theodore. Obv. arms; rev. St. Rudbart seated. 1587 to 1612. Uncirculated and beautiful. Rare. *Size, 36 x 46*

241 ———— Another. Same form for the same occasion. Fine; rare. *Size, 19 x 19*

242 LANDAU. Besieged by the French. 1713. Octagonal dollar of Charles Alexander, Duke of Wittemberg. Obv. in center, the arms of the duke, and his initials C. A. H. Z. W. surrounding; 1713; above PRO. CÆS. & IMP.; below BEL. *(agoruig)* LANDAU (Siege of Landau) 3 Fl. *(coin)* 8N (creutzets), four counter-stamps on the borders; rev. plain. **Very fine**; rare. *Size, 27 x 33*

5⁻

243 ———— Obv. a five-pointed star within a sunken shield; **below** I. P. in a suken square; rev. plain. Fine; rare. Size, 23

244 PLATE DOLLAR of Ferdinand VII. of Spain. Obv. FER VII; rev. GNA. **1808** UNDCRO. in three lines; edge and rim milled. Uncirculated; rare.

245 OCTAGONAL DOLLAR of Fer. VII. Struck during the French war. Obv. 1808 FER. VII. 1808. in three lines; rev. diamond-shaped shield. Fine. Size, 20 x 20

246 VARGAS DOLLAR. Obv. VARGAS and date 1811; rev. arms, R. CAXA DE SOMBRETE. Fair; rare.

247 SARAGOSSA. Dollar struck by the French during the siege. Obv. crowned eagle, ZARA to l. and 1813 to r. within a diamond; rev. I.O. and 4ͤ 60ᶜ in two lines within an ornamental square. Uncirculated, and *very rare*.

248 PLATE DOLLAR of Ferdinand VII. of Spain. Struck for Barcelona during the revolution. Obv. FR⁰ VII, to l. and r.; above 1821; below 30 SOUS; rev. diamond-shaped shield; below SALUS POPULI; edge and rims milled. Fine.

249 CUT MONEY OF THE ISLAND OF TRINIDAD. Very curious; rare.
3 pieces

The government cut a piece out of the centre of the coins and made the rim pass for the full value of the piece, and the part cut out for as much more.

250 BULLET MONEY OF SIAM. $\frac{1}{2}$, $\frac{1}{4}$, $\frac{1}{8}$, and $\frac{1}{16}$ tical.   4 pieces

---

Russia and Poland.

251 PETER I. ALEXOWITZ. (The Great). 1682 to 1725. Crown. Obv. bust in armor, head laureated; rev. cross, 1723. Uncirculated; rare.

252 CATHERINE I. (Mother of Peter II.) 1725-1727. Crown. Obv. bust to left, head crowned, and hair bound with fillets of pearls; rev. double-headed eagle, 1725. Broad fine crown.
Size, 27

253 ANNA IVANOVNA. 1730-1740. Crown, 1732. Obv. young bust to right, head crowned, hair in long curls; rev. double-headed eagle. Fine; very rare.

254 ELIZABETH I., PETROVNA. Crown of 1758. Obv. bust, head crowned, hair in long curls; rev. double-headed eagle. Uncirculated.

255 —— Obv. bust richly dressed, hair bound with fillets of pearls; rev. same as last, 1756. Uncirculated.

256 PETER III. 1762. Crown. Obv. bust in armor; rev. same. Uncirculated; rare.

257 CATHERINE II. Crown of 1769. Obv. bust richly dressed; rev. same. Fine.

258 NICHOLAS I. Ruble of 1845. Uncirculated.

259 SIGISMUND III. (Poland). 1587-1632. Obv. figure of the king to the waist, richly dressed and wearing ruffled collar, holding in his right hand a sword, and in his left a globe; rev. arms on a square shield crowned and encircled by the Order of the Golden Fleece. Uncirculated; rare.

Bavaria.

260 LOUIS I. 1828. Crown. Obv. bare head; rev. diademed head of his queen in an oval, surrounded by the heads of her eight children in ovals. Uncirculated.

261 —— Struck to commemorate the coronation of his son as King of Greece. Same condition.

2

ENGLAND.

Sole Monarchy.

262 EADRED. 953. Obv. EADRED. REX, a cross in center; rev. HUNE-EDMO, three pellets above and below inscription, and three crosses between. Very fine and rare.

263 CANUTE. 1017. Head with sceptre; rev. cross with circle and dot in each angle. Fine; rare.

264 EDWARD THE CONFESSOR. 1042. Bust to right with sceptre. EDWARD REX; rev. cross. Very fine; rare.

Anglo-Norman.

265 WM. I. (Conqueror). 1066. Head, full face, with crown and sceptre; rev. PAXS and cross. Very fine; scarce.

266 HENRY I. 1100. Head crowned, sceptre to left; rev. crescents within angles of cross. Fine; extremely rare.

267 HENRY II. 1154. Full face crowned, sceptre to left; rev. double cross, and four pellets in each angle. Fine.

268 RICHARD I. (Cœur-de-Lion). A.D. 1189. RICARDUS a round cross; rev. PIC TAVIENSIS. Struck at Aquitaine. Very fine; rare.

269 JOHN. 1199. King's head in a triangle, JOHANNES REX; rev. crescent in triangle. Fine; rare.

270 ——— Head front face; rev. cross with circles in the four angles. Very fine and rare.

271 HENRY III. 1216. Head; rev. long cross. Fine.

272 EDWARD I. 1272. Pattern groat. Head, front face, crowned with a *crown fleurie*, and the draperies at the neck fastened with a rosette; the whole bust enclosed in a *quatrefoil* compartment, surrounded by the legend EDWARDVS DE GRA REX ANGL; rev. *cross fleurie* with three pellets in the angles extending to the edge; around the pellets is the inscription LONDONE CIVI; the exterior legend is DNS HIB NIE DVX AQVI. Has been gilt; the rev. still retaining the traces. Very fine, and *excessively rare*.

The groat was first struck for circulation during the reign of Edward III., only patterns being struck during the reign of Edward I. This piece was in the Pembroke collection.

273 ——— London penny. Obv. head full face, crowned. EDWR-ANGLDX; rev. cross extending through the legend. Fine.

274 ——— Canterbury penny. Fine.

275 ——— Anglo Gallic. Obv. head full face, crowned, on a rose; rev. VILLA CALISIA, long cross with three pellets in angles. Very fine and rare. See Folke.

276 EDWARD II. 1307. London penny. Good.

277 EDWARD III. 1327. Penny. Head ; rev. long cross. London.
    Fine.

278 —— Groat. York. Fine.

279 —— London groat. Fair.

280 —— Another. Broader type. Fine.

281 RICHARD II. 1377. Groat. Head crowned ; rev. CIVITAS
    LONDON, cross extending through the legend, three pellets
    in each angle of the cross. Fair ; very rare. Cost £1.

282 —— York penny. Crowned head ; rev. CIVITAS EBORAC,
    long cross with three pellets in each angle. Fine ; very rare.

283 HENRY IV. OR V. 1399-1413. London groat. Very good.

284 —— Calais groat. Fine.

285 —— London penny and half-penny. Fine.   2 pieces

286 HENRY V. 1413. Calais groat. Very good.

287 —— London penny and half-penny.   2 pieces

288 HENRY VI. 1422. Calais groat. Fine.

289 —— York penny.

290 —— London half-penny.

291 EDWARD IV. 1461. Waterford groat. Fine ; scarce.

292 —— London groat. Fine.

293 —— York groat. Very fine.

294 —— Irish groat. Obv. three crowns within circle ; rev. cross
    and shield bearing arms of England and France. Fine ; rare.

295 —— York half-penny, struck for Archb. Geo. Nevill. Fine.
    Rare. See Hawkins, page 116.

296 HENRY VII. 1483. London groats, first and second coinage.
    Fine.   2 pieces

297 HENRY VIII. 1509. Groat, first coinage, exactly like the
    last coinage of Henry VII., profile to r. Very fine.

298 —— Groat, second coinage. Very fine.

299 —— Irish groat, struck for Jane Seymour. Harp, H. and J.
    crowned. Good.

300 —— Tower groat. Good for this coin. Hawkins, 396.

301 —— *Chaise penny.* Obv. the king seated in a chair holding
    sceptre and goblet ; rev. arms of England and France. Not
    fine ; *very rare.*

302 —— Durham penny. T. W. (Thomas Wolsey) on rev. Rare.
    Hawkins, 131.

303 —— Durham penny, struck for Abp. Cuthbert Tonstall.
    Rare.

304 EDWARD VI. 1547. Crown. Obv. the king on horseback
    with a sword in his hand ; his horse caparisoned ; the date,
    1551, under him ; rev. arms quartered by a cross.
    This is a fine example of the first English crown. Rare.

305 EDWARD VI. Shilling. Obv. crowned bust facing to L., rose to R. XII.; rev. arms on a shield quartered; no date. Fine; the rev. especially sharp and fine. Scarce.

306 —— Sixpence. Sharp and fine, but has an abrasion across the face. Very desirable.

307 MARY. 1553. Shilling. Obv. bust crowned, flowing hair and necklace. MARIA D.G. ANG. FRA. Z. HIB. RAGIN; rev. crowned harp, M. and R. crowned; VERITAS + TAMDORIS FILLIA: MDLIII. Nearly proof impression; has a fine brown patina. Excessively rare. Cost £3 in London many years ago, and is now worth much more.

308 —— Groat. Bust crowned; rev. " Veritas Temporis Filia." Good; rare.

309 PHILIP AND MARY. 1554. Shilling. Obv. heads of Philip and Mary under a crown, 1555; rev. harp, P and M crowned, and shield bearing arms of England, Ireland, and Scotland crowned. Very rare.

310 —— Shilling. Obv. same as last ; rev. arms crowned. Good ; very rare.

311 —— Groat. Obv. bust of Mary; rev. POSVIMVS DEVM AVDIVTO, NOS. Good; very rare.

312 ELIZABETH. 1559. Crown. Bust in profile; sceptre in right hand, and globe in left ; rev. arms, POSVI DEVM ADIVTOREM MEVM. Sharp and brilliant. One of the finest ever offered in New York. Very rare.

313 —— Half-crown to match. Equally fine; very rare.

314 —— Shilling. MM. cross. Fine ; very broad (size 2½) ; very rare.

315 —— Another MM. hand. Fine ; rare.

316 —— Shilling. MM. harp ; rev. three harps on a shield crowned, 1561. Fine and very rare.

317 —— Milled sixpence without inner circle. Rare.

318 —— Sixpence, different MM.   2 pieces

319 —— Threepence (rose). Good ; rare.

320 —— Penny. Obv. bust of the queen, head crowned, and three-quarter face. PLEDGE OF THE ; rev. cypher of the queen's name beneath crown ; A PENNY, 1601. Thick coin, size 12. Fine, but pierced ; very rare.

English Coins after the Union.

321 JAMES I. 1602. Crown. Obv. king on horseback, carrying in his hand a sword ; rev. arms on a garnished shield, with a motto, used for the first time, allusive to the union of the two crowns, QUÆ DEUS CONJUNXIT MEMO SEPARET. Extremely fine and sharp ; very rare.

322 JAMES I. Half-crown. Fine.

323 —— Another. Fair.

324 —— Shilling. MM. thistle. Fine.

325 —— Another; rev. harp. Good.

326 —— Sixpence. Good.

327 CHARLES I. 1625. Crown. **Obv.** the king on horseback with a raised sword in his hand. In good preservation, slightly pierced and filed, not injuring the coin. Nearly uncirculated. Rare.

328 —— Another variety. Fine.

329 —— Half-crown. Aberystwith mint. MM. Welsh feathers. Fine; rare.

330 —— Half-crown. Tower mint MM. crown. Nearly uncirculated, but struck on a poor planchet.

331 —— Shilling. MM. thistle. Very good; rare.

332 —— Others different mint marks; desirable. 2 pieces

333 —— Shilling. MM. (P). Nearly uncirculated; rare.

Lincoln & Son, of London, sold this to Mr. Snow for 25s., and said it was very rare.

334 —— Milled Sixpence. Fine and sharp; abrased on the face and shield, but otherwise a very desirable piece.

335 —— Another. Better than fair.

336 —— Full set Maundy money, viz.: 4d, 3d, 2d, and 1d. Fine and rare. 4 pieces

337 THE COMMONWEALTH. 1649. Crown. **Obv.** cross of St. George between a branch of palm and laurel; rev. cross and harp side by side in a double escutcheon, GOD WITH US. 1653. Very fine; rare.

338 —— Half-crown. Fine; rare.

339 —— Shilling. 1656. Fine; rare.

340 —— Twopence. Fine; rare.

341 —— Penny. Fine; rare.

342 —— Half-penny. Fine; rare.

343 OLIVER CROMWELL. Crown. 1658. **Obv.** laureated bust to left; rev. shield surmounted by crown bearing the arms of Great Britain, PAX QUÆRITUR BELLO. Very fine; almost uncirculated; rare.

344 —— Half-crown. Fine proof; very rare.

345 CHARLES II. 1660. Half-crown or thirty-pence. **Obv.** head crowned, XXX behind head; rev. arms. CHRISTO, AUSPICE REGNO. Crowned head to left. Dies by Simon. Fine; very rare.

This piece was sent by Lincoln & Son to Mr. Snow at a high price, with a recommendation to buy, as *it was very rare.*

346 CHARLES II. Shilling. MM. crown, same type. Fine; rare.

347 —— Shilling. Obv. laureated head; rev. cross bearing the arms of England, Scotland, Ireland and France; between each angle of cross two C' interlinked, MAG. BRI. FRA. ET HIBREX. Fine; rare.

348 —— Sixpence. Same type. Equally fine; rare.

349 —— Full set of Maundy money. Dies by Simon. Crowned head. Seated. **4 pieces**

350 —— Another set. Laureated head. Proof. **4 pieces**

351 JAMES II. 1685. Half-crown. Uncirculated. *Splendid,* in this condition rare.

352 —— Full set Maundy money. Proof. Very rare. **4 pieces**

353 WILLIAM AND MARY. 1689. Crown. Obv. laureated heads accolated; rev. arms in the shape of a cross, WM in angles. Fine for the piece; rare.

354 —— Half-crown. Same type. Uncirculated. Very rare in this condition.

355 —— Another; rev. plain shield. Brilliant.

356 —— Sixpence. Arms in form of a cross, WM in angles. Uncirculated.

357 —— Full set of Maundy money. Fine. 4 pieces

358 WILLIAM alone. 1695. Crown. Uncirculated and brilliant. Very rare.

359 —— Half-crown. Equally fine.

360 —— Pattern farthing. Obv. bust, "Gulielmus Tertius;" rev. Britannia seated, "Britannia." Fine and rare.

361 —— Sixpence. Uncirculated. Rare.

362 —— Another. Very nearly as fine.

363 —— Full set of Maundy money. 4 pieces

364 ANNA. 1703. Crown. Uncirculated and perfect excepting a scratch in the planchet behind the neck. Very rare.

365 —— Crown; rev. roses and plumes. Struck in Wales. Uncirculated; rare.

Ordered from Lincoln at a cost of £1 5s.

366 —— Half-crown. Same rev. as preceding. Equally fine; rare.

367 —— Half-crown. Vigo under the bust. Almost uncirculated; rare.

368 —— Shilling; rev. roses and plumes. Fine.

370 —— Another; different rev. Fine.

371 —— Sixpence. VIGO under the bust. Proof; very rare.

372 —— Another. Rev. roses and plumes. Uncirculated. Rare.

373 —— Full set of Maundy money. Three proofs. 4 pieces

374 GEORGE I. 1714. Crown. Obv. laureated bust; rev. arms on four shields arranged in the form of a cross; roses and plumes in the angles. Edge lettered; very fine.

376 GEORGE I. 1714. Half crown, S. S. C. (South Sea Company). Fair.

377 —— Shilling. Same type as last. Fine.

378 —— Sixpence. Same type as last. Fine.

379 GEORGE II. Crown. Obv. laureated bust in Roman style; rev. arms on four shields, arranged in the form of a cross; four roses in the angles. Lettered edge. Uncirculated and brilliant; very rare.

380 —— Another. Roses and plumes on rev. Fine.

381 —— Half crown; LIMA under the bust. Uncirculated and brilliant; rare.

382 —— Another. Four roses on rev. Very fine.

383 —— Shilling. Almost uncirculated.

384 —— Another. Lima under the bust. Same condition as last.

385 —— Sixpence. Same type as last; fine.

386 —— Another. Rev. four roses in angles of cross. Uncirculated and brilliant; rare.

387 —— Another. Rev. roses and plumes. Fair.

388 —— Another. Rev. four plumes. Almost uncirculated.

389 —— Full set of Maundy money. Splendid proof. 4 pieces

390 GEORGE III. 1760. Crown. Obv. laureated bust. 1818; rev. St. George and the dragon. HONI SOIT QUI MALY PENSE. Brilliant proof; very rare. By *Pistrucci.*

391 —— Bank of England dollar, 1804. Very fine.

392 —— Half crown of 1817. BRITANNIARUM, etc. Edge milled. Uncirculated.

393 —— Shilling, 1816. Fine.

396 —— Bank token. Tenpence, Irish. Uncirculated.

397 —— Sixpence, 1787. Almost uncirculated. Crowns in the angles of the cross.

398 —— Set Maundy money. Young head, 1795. Proof. 4 pieces

399 —— Another set, 1800. Proof. 4 pieces

400 —— Half-dollar of Sierra Leone Co. Uncirculated.

401 GEORGE IV. 1826. Crown. Obv. laureated bust of the king to left; rev. St. George and the dragon, 1821. By *Pistrucci.* Brilliant proof; rare.

402 —— Half-crown. Obv. same as last; rev. shield under a crown, bearing the arms of England, Ireland, Scotland, and Hanover. On either side a thistle and trefoil, and beneath a rose. ANNO, 1820. By *Pistrucci.* Very fine.

403 —— Sixpence. Brilliant proof.

404 —— Set of Maundy money, 1826. Proof. 4 pieces

405 WILLIAM IV. 1830. Set of Maundy money. Proof. 4 pieces

406 VICTORIA. 1837. Crown. Obv. head. By Wyon. Rev. crowned shield inclosed between two laurel branches, crossed; the
rose, thistle, and shamrock beneath. Botanniarum, etc.
Very fine and scarce.

407 —— Proof of 1839. Uncirculated.

408 —— Model crowns.   Two varieties.   2 pieces

409 —— Set of Maundy money.   4 pieces

Coins of Scotland.

410 DAVID I. 1124. Penny. Crowned head and sceptre to l.; rev.
cross and stars of six points. SCOTTORVM REX. Uncirculated and *very* rare.

411 ALEX. II. 1214. Penny. Crowned head and sceptre to l.;
rev. same as last. Fine; rare.

412 ALEX. III. 1249. Penny. Same description; rude; rare.

413 DAVID II. 1329. Groat. Head and sceptre to left; rev. cross
and stars of five points. VILLA EDINBVRGH. *Fine*; rare.

414 ROBERT II. 1371. Groat. Quite similar in type to last; not
as fine. Struck at Perth.

415 ROBERT III. 1390. Groat. Front face, crowned, without
sceptre; rev. same arrangement of cross and circles, but with
three *pellets* instead of stars in each angle of the cross.
VILLA EDINBVRGH. Fine and rare.

416 JAMES II. 1437. Groat. Full face crowned, with sceptre;
rev. cross, etc., in opposite angles of the cross, three pellets
and fleur-de-lis. VILLA EDINBVRGH. Fine; rare.

417 JAMES IV. 1460. Groat. Three-quarter face crowned, without
sceptre; rev. cross, with a crown and four pellets in angles.
Fine; rare.

418 JAMES V. 1513. Groat. Side-face, open crown. JACOBVS
5; rev. the Scotch shield on a cross. OPPIDVM EDIN-
BVRGI. Very fine and rare.

419 —— Billon Plack.

420 MARY. 1542. Billon plack. Thistle crowned, M-R; rev. St.
Andrew's cross, with a crown in the centre. Rare.

421 —— Testoon 1557. Scotch shield with M-R on either side;
"Maria Dei. G. Scotor Regina;" rev. cross with crosslets,
"Virtute tua libera m, 1557." Fine. Rare.

422 JAMES VI. 1567. Thistle-mark. Arms crowned; rev. a thistle
crowned. Very fine and rare.

423 —— Quarter thistle-mark. Obv. thistle; rev. cross in shape
of an X, with a crown around the centre, on either side a
fleur-de-lis. OPPIDVM EDINBVRGH. Fine and rare.

424 —— Eighth of a thistle-mark. Obv. arms crowned; rev. thistle
crowned. Fair; rare.

425 CHARLES I. 1635. Twenty-pence. Obv. head to left, crowned. XX behind the head. CAR. D.G. SCOT. ANG. FR. ET. HIB. R.; rev. thistle crowned. IVSTITIA THRONVM FIRMAT. Fine and exceedingly rare.

Medals.

426 CHILI, 1799. Obv. arms, lion crowned within a triple shield beneath a crown; below, implements and objects of agriculture, commerce, and war. GLORIOSA. STEMMATA. REGNI CHILENSIS; rev. inscription in fourteen lines. Proof. Splendid medal. Size, 37

427 ALLIANCE MEDAL. BETWEEN PETER I. (the Great) of Russia and Charles Christian of Brunswick and Luneburg. Obv. their busts jugate; rev. two hands clasped above an altar bearing two shields with arms of Russia and Brunswick, and a blazing fire. NON VSQ. VAM. etc. Somewhat nicked. Rare. Size, 30

428 " PRESENTED BY THE CITY OF NEW YORK to the N. Y. Regiment of Volunteers in Mexico." Fine proof, by *Wright.* Size, 33

429 MEDAL STRUCK in honor of the advancement of M. de la Michodiere. 1776. Obv. his arms supported by two greyhounds; rev. arms of Paris. Fine and rare. Size, 20

430 CLEMENT XI. 1707. Obv. bust to left; rev. the Pope kneeling at the foot of a rock, on the top of which is an " Agnes Dei," behind the Pope a female with palm branch and anchor. Fine old medal. Size, 28

431 BERN MONNIER, CANTON ARGAU. St. Michiel slaying the dragon; rev. coat of arms, with plumed helmet. Very fine. Size, 21

432 JOHN WILLIAM, DUKE OF SAXONY. Obv. laureated head; rev. Spanish galley. Size, 16

433 CORONATION MEDAL OF MARIA THERESE AND FRANCIS II., 1742. Obv. sceptre and olive branch crossed under a crown. Fine proof. Size, 13

434 COMMEMORATIVE MEDAL OF THE SECOND CENTENARY OF THE AUGSBURG CONFESSION. On one side representations of the birth of Jesus, an open Bible and lighted candle, the sacrament, an angel, eagle, lion, and bull, in ex. MEM. JVBIL. II AVG. CONF.; rev. an altar, above it an angel flying, with an open book; in ex. XXV IVN. MDCCXXX. Slightly injured proof. A very beautiful and rare medal. Size, 28

435 MEDAL CROWN OF THE CITY OF NUREMBURG. Fine view of the city. 1754. Very fine.

436 MEDAL OF THE TOWN OF MÜNSTER. Struck by the Ministery of Westphalia. View of the town above. MONAS TERIVM. A hand issuing from the clouds holding a palm and olive branch, below WESTPHALI.; rev. two hands issuing from the clouds and clasped. GEDACTNVS DES ALLGEMEINEN FRIEDEN SCHLVSS IN MVNSTER. 1648. Very fine and rare. Size 26

437 RATISSBURG. Crown of the Republic of Ratisbon, with a view of the city, 1754. Uncirculated and splendid.

438 RELIGIOUS MEDAL. On one side Jacob lying asleep, a ladder reaching to heaven, with angels passing up and down ; rev. Jacob pouring oil on the stone. See Gen. xxviii. 12, 18. Fine old medal in frame of wire rope. Gilt. Rare. Size 31

439 COMMEMORATIVE MEDAL of the foundation of the University of Heidelberg, 1386—third Jubilee, 1646. Three figures in a gothic edifice ; rev. inscription in thirteen lines. Extremely fine, very rare. Size 27

440 RELIGIOUS MEDAL. Obv. Christ seated blessing little children. ER. SEGNETE SIE ; rev. goblet and book on a pulpit, encircled by a serpent holding his tail in his mouth ; in ex. ZUR ERINNERUNG. Splendid proof. Size 25

441 PROCLAMATION MEDAL OF ITURBIDE. Obv. bare bust ; rev. inscription in five lines. 1825. Proof ; rare. Size 25

442 COMMEMORATIVE DOLLAR OF LOUIS I. OF BAVARIA. 1833. Struck to commemorate the treaty between Bavaria and Nuremberg. Proof. Size 24

443 MORTUARY MEDAL. Crown of John Frederick of Brunswick and Luneburg. 1679. Obv. coat of arms with five crests ; rev. inscription in thirteen lines. Fine and rare. Size 29

444 MEDAL OF JAMES, DUKE OF YORK. Struck to commemorate his baptism. Obv. arms, NON SIC MILI E COHORTES ; rev. within a beautiful wreath of a rose and thistle branch JACOBVS DVX EBOR. NAT. 15 OCT. BAPTIZ. 24 NOVE. 1633. A gem. Proof. Size 19

445 MEDAL. Crown of NUREMBERG. 1768. Obv. arms ; rev. view of the city. Proof.

446 PROCLAMATION MEDAL OF ITURBIDE. Obv. military bust ; rev. two wolves rearing against a tree, GUADA LAXARA. EN VENTUROSA. PROCLAMACION 1822. Very fine and rare. Size 25

447 PAPAL MEDAL. Obv. bust of Gregory XVI. ; rev. baptismal scene. Uncirculated. Size 24

448 BAPTISMAL MEDAL. Obv. St. John the Baptist baptizing Christ ; above, the rays of the sun, " This is my beloved Son," in German, and a dove descending from heaven. Quotations from John i. and Math. iii. ; on the margin, quotation from Matt. xxiii. ; rev. WER GLAVBT, etc. March, 1816 ; and quotations from the Bible in ten lines. Very fine and rare. Size 32

449 MARRIAGE MEDAL. Obv. marriage ceremony, QUOS DEUS
CONJUNXIT HOMO NON SEPARET ; rev. wedding
— feast at Cana, Christ turning the water into wine, JESUS
CHRIST MACHET WASSER ZU WEIN. IN CAN-
GAL. IOH. II. Very fine and rare. Size, 35

450 JEROME NAPOLEON AND CATHARINA, King and Queen of
Westphalia. Obv. their heads jugata ; rev. GLÜCK
AUF ! CLAUSTHAL DEN 8 AUGUST, 1811 ; below, two
hammers crossed, within a beautiful wreath. *Very fine* and
exceedingly rare. Size, 28

451 CORONATION MEDAL OF CHARLES VI., Emperor of Germany,
Maximilian Emanuel of Bavaria, and a little reward of merit
medal. All very fine. Size, 16. 3 pieces

452 MEDAL OF BREMEN. Obv. statue of Roland of Bremen ; rev.
view of the city, CONSERVA DOMINE HOSPITIUM
ECCLESIÆ. TUÆ. ; in ex. 1640. Very fine and very
rare. Size, 36

453 NUREMBERG MEDAL CROWN. Obv. three shields, "Moneta
Nova Reip Norimbergensis," 1694 ; rev. fine view of the city,
SVB VMBRA ALARVM TVARVM. Splendid ; rare.

454 REFORMATION MEDAL. Obv. busts of Luther, Churf, and
Melancthon jugata ; rev. Luther presenting his protest to
the Pope ; in ex. DEN 25 IUNII, 1530. Struck to commemorate the third centennial of Luther, 25 June, 1830.
Fine proof ; rare. Size, 25

455 ANTHONY ULRICK, Duke of Bruns. and Lune., 1700. Obv.
wild man. Very fine. Set in a border of volutes with heart
pendant and loop. Size, 26

456 MEDAL CROWN OF BASLE. Obv. arms of Basle supported by
a cockatrice. DOMINE CONSERVA NOS IN PACE ;
rev. view of the city ; in ex. BASILEA, 1793. Good. Size, 26

457 MEDAL CROWN OF LOUIS I. OF BAVARIA. Struck to commemorate his joining the Order of St. Michael, 1837. Proof.

458 "LIBERTE RECONQUISE PAR LES FRANCAIS, July 30," within
wreath ; rev. trophy of flags, arms, etc. Fine proof. Size, 17

459 REFORMATION MEDAL. 1817. Obv. bust of Martin Luther ;
rev. busts of Zwingli and Melancthon, face to face. By Loos.
Beautiful proof. Rare.

460 LUTHER MEDAL. Obv. bust, front face, in his priestly robes,
— holding an open Bible ; rev. Luther nailing his protest against
the church door ; in ex. DRITTES IUBELFEST DER
REFORMATION, AN 31 OCTOBER, 1817. Fine ; rare.
Size, 27

461 ASMI ACHMET EFFENDI. Obv. turbaned bust ; rev. inscription in 8 lines, 1791. Fine ; rare. Size, 18

462 CONQUEST OF EGYPT. Obv. pyramid ; rev. the Nile personified. Proof. Size, 21

463 ANNA, 1666. Rev: "Mutaus. Iste ardormensem," the sun reflected from two mirrors. Fine.   Size, 18

464 —— 1794. Betrothal medal. Obv. busts of Anna and Charles jugata; in ex. SPONSI ; rev. shield in front of two torches, crossed. Fine proof.   Size, 18

465 BELGIUM. Waterloo medalet, June 18, 1815. Obv. the Prince of Orange on horseback ; rev. within a beautiful wreath, WATERLOO, JUNE 18, 1815.   Proof.   Size, 16

466 MARRIAGE MEDAL OF FRANCIS JOSEPH AND ELIZABETH OF AUSTRIA.   Proof.   Size, 19

467 PROCLAMATION MEDAL OF PERU. Sun, full face ; rev. inscription in eight lines. Fine proof.   Size, 18

468 REPUBLIC OF BERNE. Rev. an artisan at work. CULTURA MITESCIT. Fine ; rare.   Size, 20

469 MEDAL OF CHARLES XIV. OF NORWAY. Obv. bust, crowned ; rev. inscription in beautiful wreath. Fine.   Size, 19

470 CORONATION MEDALS OF MARIA THERESA, 1743 ; Leopold of Austria, 1741 ; and Francis of Lorraine, 1745. Very fine little medals. Size, 15.   3 pieces

471 TEMPERANCE MEDALS. Obv. bouquet of the rose, thistle, and trefoil. UNITED WE CONQUER ; rev. a fountain surrounded by an inscription. Proof, fine.   Size, 21

472 PROCLAMATION MEDAL OF FERDINAND VII. OF SPAIN. Obv. military bust to right ; rev. arms. NOV. VERACRUZ PROCLAM. AN. 1808. Splendid proof. Rare. Size, 25

473 GEORGE WILLIAM, DUKE OF BRUNSWICK-LUNE. Obv. bust in a double circle, surrounded by fourteen shields ; rev. figures of Piety seated under a tree, and Justice with sword and scales standing ; above, a hand issuing from a cloud holding a wreath. PIETATE ET JUSTITIA. Very fine and exceedingly rare.   Size, 31

474 CORONATION MEDAL OF GEO. I. Obv. laureated head ; rev. the king seated on a throne receives the crown from Britannia ; in ex. INAVGVRAT XX OCT, 1714. Fine. Size, 22

475 RATISBON, 1754. 20 marks of the Republic under Francis I., with fine view of the city of Regensburg. Uncirculated.   Size, 25

476 MEDAL OF THE REFORMATION. Obv. bust of Earnest Louis, Landgrave of Hass ; rev. a kneeling figure before an altar on which is a smoking censer ; above, rays of the sun. FESTVM SECVLARE SECVNDVM ECCLESIAE EVANG. LA-THER, 31 OCT. 1717 ; in ex. HASSIA VOTERVM COMPOS. DEO GRATIA. Very fine. Rare.   Size, 27

477 CORONATION MEDAL OF WILLIAM IV. Obv. his bust, bare ; rev. head of Adelaide, with a coronet. Sept. 8, 1831. Splendid proof. By Wyon.   Size, 20

478 GREGORY XVI.. 1830. Obv. his bust; rev. Christ washing the
feet of one of His disciples. Fine. Size, 20

479 MEDAL OF WILLIAM III, Obv. laureated bust. THE GLORI-
OUS & IMMORTAL MEMORY, 1690; rev. arms. KING
& CONSTITUTION. By *Mossop*. Rare. Loop removed.
Size, 21

480 RELIGIOUS MEDAL. On one side, three ovals; one representing Naaman bathing in the Jordan; another, Christ baptized
by John, and the third a baptismal font; rev. three ovals;
on one, Jacob embracing Esau; another, Mary Magdalene
before Christ, and the third, baptizing a child in the blood of
Christ. With inscriptions in Dutch. Splendid proof. Rare.
Size, 28

481 PRO BONO PUBLICO. Rev. Public Happiness, 1804. Fine.

482 AUGSBURG CONFESSION MEDALET. Obv. female with cross
and book. "Confession evang. in. com. aug. exhibitae."
25 IUN; rev. arms. "Imperial civit Lubicencis, 1730."
Fine and rare. Size, 16

483 BLUCHER MEDALET. Obv. military bust. "Alex. Leop. V.
Blucher, K.P. Gener. Feld. Marshall. Geb 16 Decb, 1743;
rev. Germania seated, leaning on a shield, holding in her
hand a figure of Victory with a crown. "Des Befreiers
Schleasen;" in. ex. Sieg. A.D. Katzb, 1813" Fine; rare.
Size, 17

484 LUDWIG KÖNIG V., BAVARIA. Bust; rev. within a beautiful
wreath, "Dem wohl Verhalten und Fleisse." Proof. Size, 17

485 RELIGIOUS MEDAL. Obv. Moses receiving the tables of the
law on Mt. Sinai; rev. the two tables with the Ten Command-
ments; the serpent and apple beneath; a legend in Dutch
on the edge. Very fine; rare. Size, 25

486 SEDE VACANTE CROWN OF COLOGNE. Obv. St. Peter; rev.
the three kings, CASPAR, MELCHIOR, BALTHASAR,
paying homage to Jesus in the arms of the Virgin, 1761. Fine
and rare.

487 VERY CURIOUS AND INTERESTING OLD MEDAL, made in same
manner as preceding, but in higher relief; on one side two
females in a garden, one binding up the leg of the other;
above them is a castle, on the balcony of which appears an
old harper. rev. two women and a man in the woods,
evidently having a picnic; in the distance a City.
Very fine and rare; with loop. Size, 28

488 BAPTISMAL MEDAL. Obv. Priest baptizing a child. ALSO
DIE HEILGE TAUF UNS REIN UND SELIGMACHT;
rev. a Bible open at NUM. 17, v. 8; on a pulpit (?) across
the page is Aaron's rod. WIE AARON'S WUNDERSTAB
HAT BLUTH UND FRUCHT GEBRACHT. Without
date; but figures in the costume of the 17th Century.
Splendid proof; rare. Size, 31

489 TIEDPINK (ZURICH). Medal crown of 1728. Obv. shield supported by two lions, Moneta, etc.; rev. view of the city. Very fine.

490 GEORGE II. INDIAN MEDAL. Obv. laureated head; rev. arms within the garter supported by the lion and unicorn, surmounted by a crowned helmet on which stands a lion, crowned. Loop removed. *Very fine and rare old medal.* Size, 28

This medal resembles the Indian medal of Geo. III., especially the reverse. It does not appear to have been struck from dies, but to have been cast and carefully finished. I am under the impression that this medal was made for America during th· war, with the French.

491 COMMEMORATIVE MEDAL of Joseph I., Duke of Austria and Emperor of Germany. Bust in armor, 1727, MARI, head laureated; rev. sun rising over a beautiful landscape, man galloping. PROCEDENDO SALVTIFER CRESCET. Very fine. Size, 28

492 PROCLAMATION MEDAL of Orizava. 1790. Obv. laureated head of Charles IV. of Spain; rev. Mexican eagle, crowned, upholding the arms of Spain, and inscription. *Very fine.* Rare. Size, 25

493 CORONATION CROWN OF FRIEDBERG. 1804. MON NOV CASTRI IMP. FRIEDBERG; St. George on horseback slaying the dragon, in this distance the castle; rev. double eagle. FRANC II D.G., etc. Proof. Rare. Size, 20

494 BAPTISM MEDAL. Christ crowned with thorns, a large bust in profile; rev. His baptism by St. John; in the distance, a view of Jerusalem. Quotation from Matt. iii. *A superb and valuable medal.* Size, 29

This Rare Medal is a remarkable conception; it was from the late writer's collection, and the writer eighteen years ago saw Mr. Snowden refuse $30 for it from Father Dillon, a Catholic Priest of Philadelphia.—W. J. S.

495 COMMEMORATIVE MEDAL of THE DEDICATION of THE SALZBURG CATHEDRAL, 25 Sept. 1628. Sancta Rupertus and Virgilius upholding the cathedral; rev. four Cardinals carrying the Host. Fine and rare. Size, 22

496 COMMEMORATIVE MEDAL of THE FIRST CENTENNIAL OF THE REFORMATION JUBILEE, Oct. 31, 1517. Obv. bust of John George with drawn sword. VERBVM DOMINI MANET IN ÆTERNVM, 1617; rev. bust of Frederick III., with drawn sword. SECVLVM LVTHERANVM, 1517. Splendid uncirculated medal crown. Very rare. Size, 28

497 MEDAL OF WILLIAM, DUKE OF SAXONY. 1650. Three hands meeting above a sword, PAX ESTO, etc.; rev. two hands from the clouds holding a wreath above a coat of arms, to it a branch, 1618; to it a sword upright, 15-17; below, 1650. Uncirculated. Rare. Size, 21

498 MORTUARY MEDAL. Obv. an angel standing near a monument. DEIN GUTTER ENGEL SEY DIR STETS ZUR
SEITE. ; rev. inscription in eight lines, divided by a rod,
around which is twined a stem of lilies. Nearly proof, by
Loos. Rare. Size, 23

499 RELIGIOUS MEDAL. Obv. the infant Jesus with one foot on a
globe, transfixed by a serpent, and the other on a cloud, surrounded by clouds and angels; rev. an inscription in seven
lines within an ornamental border. Dated MDCXXVII.
Splendid proof; a gem, worth $25. Oval size, 24 x 21.
This is one of the most charming medals I ever saw; the workman-
ship is beyond all praise. It will be an ornament to any collection.

500 MEDAL OF ABERCROMBIE. 1801. For gallantry against the
French in Egypt. Engraved by *Pidgeon*, from a design by
R. West. Fine, rare, and valuable. Size, 31

501 MEDAL OF HENRY IV. OF FRANCE, struck to commemorate
the battle of Ivry. Obv. bust of the King in armor, head
laureated. HENRICVS IIII D. G. FRAN. ET. NA.
REX. rev. a crown on the point of a sword, surrounded by
olive branches and four shields, one bearing the arms of
France, another of Navarre, the other two with figures:
VICTORIA IVRICA. A splendid medal, and rare in ex-
cess. Very thick. Loop removed. Size, 31
The gentleman of whom Mr. Snow purchased this medal, assured
him that it was unique; those usually seen being re-strikes,
and so indifferently this one being genuine.

502 LOUIS XIII. Obv. a hand with a sickle reaping lilies ; NE
OFFICIENT, 1622 ; rev. arms of France and Navarre on
two shields, " Argenterie Du Roy." Fine ; rare. Size, 17

503 AUGSBURG CONFESSION. Medal to celebrate the second Centenary. bust of Christian, Duke of Saxony ; rev. Duke kneeling before him on a pulpit in open table, in the open air,
view of the country. OMNIS ERGO QVI CONFI-
TEBITVRME. In ex. MEM. IVE. II CONFESS.
FATH. EXHIB. 25. IVN. 1730. Proof. Rare. Size, 20

504 REFORMATION MEDAL. Obv. bust in cap ; BERDOLT
HALLER REFORM; rev. WIR HALTEN FEST WAS
GOTT UNS GAB; in ex. III. REFORM. FEITER IN-
BERN. 1828. Nearly proof. Rare. Size, 30

505 —— Obv. busts of Haller and Kolb. MDXXVII ; rev.
Christ between them. MANE NOBISCUM ; in ex. IV.
BIL.: II DUM. BERN. CEL. 7. IAN. 1728. Very fine;
rare. Size, 20

506 RELIGIOUS MEDAL. Obv. St. George on horseback slaying the
dragon ; in the distance a female kneeling in a rock, praying.
S. GEORGIUS EQVITVM PATRONVS; rev. Christ in
the ship sleeping during the storm ; IN TEMPESTATE
SECVRITAS. Splendid proof. Rare. Size, 28

507 Papal Medal. Obv. bust of Clement XI.; rev. three females.
DIGNIS VICTORIAM. Fine.   Size, 29

508 Medal of John Earnest, Archbishop of Salzburg. Obv.
arms; rev. Saints Rudertus and Virgilius seated, with the
Cathedral at their feet. Very fine; rare.   Size, 22

509 Episcopal Medal. Dollar of John Eucharius, Bishop of
Eichstadt. 1694. Arms with four crests ; rev. St. Willibald
standing. Uncirculated and splendid crown. Rare. Size, 27

510 Religious Medal. Meeting between Abraham and Lot.
WIR SIND GEBRRUDER. GEN. 13, v. 8. ; rev. inscription in thirteen lines. Fine.   Size, 26

511 Episcopal Medal. Dollar of Francis Arnold, Bishop of
Paderborn, 1710 ; rev. busts of Saint Liborius and Charles
the Great to the waist. Fine and rare.   Size, 27

512 Commemorative Medal. Obv. Apollo driving the steeds of
the Sun, above him section of the Zodiac with four signs.
SOLEM MENTITUR QUEM SIDERA TERRENT ;
rev. Sun rising over mountains ; in ex. STRAGES GALL.
AD MONTES HANNON XI SEPT. MDCCIX. Very
fine and rare.   Size, 27

513 Jubilee Medal. Struck to commemorate the fourth centenary of the foundation of the University at Heidelberg. Bust
of Charles Theodore ; rev. LAETA SAECVLI V. AVS-
PICIA, Pallas seated, leaning on a shield ; in ex. M. NOV
MDCCLXXXVI. HEIDELBERGAE. Proof; rare.
                                                 Size, 23

514 Commemorative Medal of Louis XV. 1745. Obv. filleted
head ; rev. the king in a quadriga, Victory crowning him
with a wreath, DECVS IMPERII GALLICI ; in ex.
HOSTES AB IPSOMET REGE FVSI AD FONTENO-
IVM XI MAII MDCCXLV. Fine.   Size 26

515 Proclamation Medal of Potosi. Obv. a mountain, surmounted by a double-headed eagle, crowned ; rev. POTOSI
PRO. FERDINANDO VII. ANNO 1808. Proof.
                                                 Size, 25

516 Commemorative Medal. Obv. bust, FROM. RUDOLPH.
PISCHEKUS DHEOLOG COBURG. NAT. AC.
MDCLXXXVII. etc. ; rev. inscription in twelve lines.
Interesting old medal.   Size, 26

517 —— Obv. head of an ox with a ring through his nose, between
two angels, UND MECKLENBURG ZUN RUH GE-
BRACHT ; in ex. GAUDIUM MECKLENBURG CIII
1701, 16 July ; rev. two houses, on opposite sides of the
river, united together by chains and padlocked, a hand issuing from a cloud holding chain, CONSOLO DATA
MEGOPOLIS, 1701, 8 MARTII. Rare and curious old
medal ; fine.   Size, 24

518 Religious Medal. Obv. David kneeling, playing on a harp,
1707, with inscription in Dutch ; rev. inscription in four
lines within a wreath.   Size, 25

519 PROCLAMATION MEDAL of Mexico, 1789. Obv. laureated head of Charles IV. of Spain, CAROLUS IV. HISP. E IND REG. MEX. PROCL.; rev. bust of Louisa, head laureated, LVDOV. REG. AUSPICE. ALF. ARCH. MEX. Fine, especially the rev. Size, 26

520 CORONATION MEDAL OF QUEEN CAROLINE. Obv. bust to left; rev. the Queen standing between Britannia and a veiled female; in ex. CORON. XI OCTOB, MDCCXXVII. Fine. Size, 22

521 MORTUARY MEDALET. Fine work; proof. Size, 16

522 FRANKLIN MEDAL. By *Wright & Bale.* Bust of Franklin, GIFT OF FRANKLIN, 1788; rev. inscription, 1839. Rare and valuable; pierced. Size, 21

523 MEDALETS OF GEORGE I. Obv. head, three-quarter face; rev. monogram: Geo. III. Obv. Britannia seated, 1796; same rev. Very fine. 2 pieces. Size, 13

524 —— Louis XV. of France, Geo. Wilhelm, Duke Brun. and Lune., and proclamation medal of Peru. All very fine. 3 pieces. Size, 18

525 QUAINT OLD DUTCH MEDAL. On one side three men in armor joining hands; rev. partially draped female leaning on a broken column; behind her a lion with loop. Gilt. Rare. Size, 23

526 —— On one side a man standing in front of a seated woman, holding a mirror, " Ich ehre was du fühlst;" rev. two men conversing, " Gut dak du mich nicht fliehst." Fine; rare. Size, 21

527 CISALPINE REPUBLIC. Obv. female with helmet and spear seated, also a female standing, at her feet a cornucopia, behind her a stork; rev. inscription in oak wreath. Proof. Size, 25

528 " FIDELITE BONHEUR." Male and female figures in Roman costume; rev. "CG 8. 9bre 1834," within a beautiful wreath of flowers. By *Petit.* Proof. Size, 21

529 DUTCH MEDAL. Obv. a group of figures under a tree; rev. AAN JAN HEND. WEENINK 4 SEPT., 1855, in oak wreath, and inscription in Dutch surrounding. Fine. Size, 28

Coins of the Sequestrated Cities of Germany.

530 AUSTRIA. Silver coins of Leopold, Francis, Ferdinand II. and III., and Rudolph. Fine and rare lot. Size, 13. 5 pieces

531 CHRISTIAN IV. of Denmark, 1588. Cardinal Francis of Constanz, 1761, and Charles Joseph of Fürstenberg, 1804. Fine. Av. size, 17. 5 pieces

2

532 FREDERICK EARNEST of Bruns and Lune., 1639; Ferdinand II., 1628, struck for Cologne; Maximilian II. of Magdeburg; Charles XI. of Sweden, and others. Fine lot. Size, 15.
10 pieces

533 TEUTONIC ORDER. Coins of 1544, 1546, 1680, and one early one undated. Fine and rare. Av. size, 14. 4 pieces

534 —— Double Groschen of Walram, 1341. Very fine ; rare. Size, 16

535 —— Others. Saint Ursus, 1550, Saint Peter, Treves, and another. Fine and rare lot. Size, 17. 5 pieces

536 SAINT LEOPOLD of Lucerne, 1634 ; Saint Killanus, 1679 ; Saint Martin, 1624, and others. Fine lot. Size, 14.
10 pieces

537 BISHOPRIC OF MINDEN, 1576-8, 1634, and one undated ; Magdeburg, 1623. Rare and valuable lot. Size, 16. 6 pieces

538 ERFURT, 1622 and 1623 ; Magdeburg, 1612 ; Minden, 1580, 1623 and others. Fine lot; rare. Size, 14. 10 pieces

539 LUBECK. Early pennies. "Moneta Lubicencis ;" rev. "Cross Civitas Imperial." Fine and rare. Size, 12. 3 pieces

540 —— Another lot. Size, 12. 3 pieces

541 BRACTEATES OF THE THIRTEENTH CENTURY. Very fine and rare. 5 pieces

542 EARLY PENNIES of Prussia, Saxony, and Bremen. Very valuable lot. 6 pieces

543 NUREMBERG : Matthias, 1615 ; Magdeburg, 1619 and 1622 ; Charles of Lichtenstein, 1690, and others. Fine lot. Size, 14. 10 pieces

544 EARLY PENNIES and Bracteates of Halle, Bruns. and Lune., Furstenburg, and others. Rare lot. 10 pieces

545 EARLY GROATS of Austria ; Philip, Count of Flanders, 1571 ; Maximilian, Emperor of Germany, struck for Isny, and others. Valuable lot. Size, 16. 5 pieces

546 SELECTED Lot of small German coins. Good. Size, 10.
10 pieces

547 —— of Poland, and coins struck by Holland for India. Size, 14. 10 pieces

548 GEORGE WILLIAM of Bruns. and Lune., 1691 ; Rudolph, Emperor, and others. Fine lot. Av. size, 16. 15 pieces

549 SELECTED Lot of early coins. Some rare ; very interesting and desirable lot. Size, 13. 10 pieces

550 —— of early groats and old German pennies. Good lot ; some rare. 10 pieces

551 CHARLES V., Austria, 1553 ; Maximilian I. ; Theodore Adolph, Bishop of Paderborn, 1655, and others. Rare and interesting lot. Size, 16. 10 pieces

552 Medalets and small coins. Good lot. Size, 12. 10 pieces

553 Selected Lot of Cantons. Vaud, Luzern, Bern, Zurich, St.
    Galen, Argau, Glarns, Geneva, Basel. Desirable lot. Size,
    16.   10 pieces

554 —— Another lot; different.   20 pieces

Foreign Crowns, Medals, etc.

555 Two-third Crown of Lubeck. 1549. Double eagle,
    MONETA, etc.; rev. St. John with lamb and cross. Coun-
    terstamped. Fine and rare.

556 Holland. Crown. 1589. Soldier standing, his legs con-
    cealed by a shield; rev. lion rampant, and inscription. Very
    rare old crown. Poor.

557 Christian IV. of Denmark. 1617. Figure of the king to
    the waist; rev. shield with three lions, "1 Marck Danske,"
    (40 cents). Fine.

558 Philip IV. of Spain. 1636. Crown. Bust to r.; rev. arms.
    Ordinary.

559 Christian IV. of Denmark. Ducat of 1645. Obv. C⁴ be-
    neath a crown; rev. JUSTUS JUDEX, and Hebrew char-
    acters. Fine and rare.

560 Charles V. of Germany. Crown of 1659. Figure of the
    emperor with sword and hand; rev. arms. Poor; rare.

561 Earnest Augustus of Bruns. and Lune. "XII Marien
    Gros. of 1670. Obv. helmet surmounted by a horse and
    feather. Augustus of Saxony (?) ½ crown; Frederick
    William ½ crown. Fine lot.   3 pieces

562 Francis I., Count of Mansfeld. ½ crown of 1671. St.
    George and dragon; rev. arms. Gilt; fine; rare.

563 Max. Henry (Bavaria), Archbishop of Cologne. Crown of
    1671. Bust, head bare; rev. arms. Ordinary; rare.

564 Geo. William of Brun. and Lune. 1675. "XII Marien
    Grosch"; rev. horse galloping. Fine.

565 Philip William of Bavaria. Crown of 1675. Bust, curly
    hair; rev. arms. Fine and rare.

566 Rudolph Augustus, Bruns. and Lune. Wild man; rev.
    "XII Marien Gros," 1676. Fine; rare.

567 Holland. Half-crown of 1685. Soldier standing, one leg
    behind a shield; rev. three shields. Fine; rare.

568 Frederick William of Bavaria. Crown of 1688. Bust;
    rev. arms. Fair; scarce.

569 Netherlands. Pieces of 6 stivers (quarter-dollar size) of
    Magensis, Daventria, Campen, and another. Knight gal-
    loping; rev. lion on a shield, etc. Good lot.   6 pieces

570 Maximilian Emanuel of Bavaria. Broad crown of 1694.
Bust, hair in long curls; rev. Virgin and Child, and inscription. Uncirculated.

571 Austria. Leopold. Bust, rev. arms 1694; rev. Virgin and Child, " Patrona Hungariæ," 1674, and another. Good lot. 3 pieces.   Size, 30

572 Frederick I. of Prussia. Crown of 1702. Bust; rev. arms crowned. Fair.

573 George II., Brun. and Lune. ½ crown, 1754. Arms; rev. St. Andrew. Charles VI. of Germany; 1726; arms; rev. castle, " Hamburger Currentgelde," and another.   4 pieces

574 Stolberg. Christian Louis, " XXIV Marien Groschen," 1740. Fine.

575 Anhalt. John Louis and Christina Augustus. ¾ crown. Their busts jugata, facing right; rev. arms, " Fratrum Concordia," 1742. Fine.

576 Austria. Maria Theresia. 1745. ⅔ crown, struck for Hungary. Uncirculated.

577 Lubeck. Crown of 1752. Uncirculated.

578 Clement XII. 1761. Arms; rev. St. Peter and St. Paul; rev. inscription. Size, 10.   2 pieces

579 " Frederick Borussorum " of Prussia, and Francis of Austria. Uncirculated. Size, 28.   2 pieces

580 Lippe-Schaumberg. William I. ⅔ crown. 1761. Bust, under it a rose; rev. arms. Rare.   2 pieces

581 Charles, Duke of Brunswick and Lune. Crown of 1765. Bust; rev. horse galloping. Fine.

582 Alexander of Brandenburg. Crown of 1765. Bust; rev. arms; and one of Maximilian of Austria. Fine. 2 pieces

583 Convention Crown of Frankfort. 1767. Obv. eagle crowned; rev. cross and inscription. Fine.

584 Ducatoon of the Republic of Ragusa. 1767. Bust in wig; rev. shield crowned, with sword and sceptre crossed behind. crown. Rare; fine.

585 Belgian Confederacy. 1790. Crown. Obv. knight on horseback galloping to r., under the horse a coat of arms , rev. arms upheld by two lions, etc. Almost uncirculated.

586 Episcopal Medal. 1770. Obv. female in armor, with three cherubs about her; rev. arms. With loop. Fine. Size, 20

587 Rome. Pius VI. 1778. Arms; rev. Virgin Mary holding keys, AVXILIVM DE SANCTO. Uncirculated. Size, 21

588 Crown of Jerome, Bishop of Austria, etc. 1784. Obv. bust in robes; rev. arms on a crowned ermine; behind a crozier and sword crossed. Very good; rare.

589 Tuscany. Leopold I. 1787. Scudo. Bust; rev. crowned shield with arms of Austria, Lotharingia, and Tuscany, with Order and Chain of Golden Fleece and Star of Maria Theresa. Very good; rare.

590 CHARLES IV. OF SPAIN. 1789. Arms crowned ; rev. double-
headed eagle crowned, bearing a shield with three crowns,
K-I, and a flower beneath, on either side the pillars crowned,
" Public Fidelit Jurant D 10 octobius." Uncirculated : rare.
Size, 23

591 TUSCANY. Ferdinand III. 1793. Scudo. Bust ; rev. shield
as above, " Veritas lex Qua." Good ; rare.

592 BASLE. 1793. View of city in ex., " Basilea"; rev. arms
supported by a cockatrice and motto. Fine.

593 GENOA. ½ crown of 1794. Obv. shield bearing a cross, supported by two winged griffons, " Dux et Gub. Reip. Genu ";
rev. St. John the Baptist, " Non Surrexit Major." Pierced ;
good ; rare.

594 AUSTRIA. Francis II. 1797. ⅔ crown. Bust ; rev. orna-
mented cross, in the angles three crowns, and the Order of
the Golden Fleece. Struck for Brabant. Fine.

595 GEORGE IV. ¼ crown. 1803. Struck for Bruns. and Lune.
Bust ; rev. arms. Uncirculated.

596 SPAIN. Ferdinand IV. 1805. Dollar. Bust to r.; rev. arms.
Fair.

597 HAMBURG. 32 Schillinge Courant, 1808 ; rev.arms, " 17 Eine
Mark Fine." Uncirculated.

598 PRUSSIA. Frederick William III. Thaler. Military bust to l.;
rev. arms, etc. Poor.

599 BAVARIA. Dollar of Max. Joseph, 1817. Obv. laureated
head ; rev. " Charta Magna Bavaria." Proof.

600 —— Louis I. 1827. Bare bust ; rev. cross in wreath of lilies. To commemorate his receiving the Order of Maria
Therese. Uncirculated.

601 —— 1833. To commemorate a treaty between Bavaria and
Prussia, Saxony, Hesse-Cassel, and Thuringia. Uncirculated.

602 BERN MUNSTER, Canton Argau. St. Michael slaying the
dragon ; rev. arms. Fine. Size, 29

603 WILLIAM IV. 1833. ⅔ crown, struck for Hanover. Uncirculated.

604 WIRTEMBURG, William I. 1841. Obv. laureated head; rev.
seated female, etc. Half-dollar. Fair.

605 SAXONY. Frederick Augustus. Bust ; rev. " Vollendet D. 4
Mai, 1827." Uncirculated. Size, 18

606 WILLIAM II. Fulda. " 6 Einen Thaler." Very good.

607 FERDINAND I. OF AUSTRIA. 1848. Obv. laureated bust ;
rev. Virgin and Child. Uncirculated and fine. Struck for
Hungary. Size, 14 and 17. 2 pieces

608 PRUSSIA. Thaler. 1861. Obv. William and Augusta, their
busts jugata. Uncirculated.

609 EARNEST, DUKE OF SAXE-COBURG-GOTHA. 1832. Medal. Obv.
bare bust to l.; rev. inscription in eight lines within an oak
wreath. Fine. Size, 21

610 OCTAGONAL MEDAL. Obv. the Archangel Michael slaying
the dragon, on a shield crowned ; rev. S. P. Q. R. within an
oak wreath. **Fine.**   Size, 20

611 SILVER MEDALET OF LUCERNE. 1793. Arms; rev. cross and inscription enclosed in a rim with loop and pendant.   Size, 14

612 RELIGIOUS MEDALETS. Virgin Mary and inscription ; rev.
cross, M, two hearts, etc.; oval. Size, 13 and 10.   2 pieces

613 DUTCH MEDALET. Shepherd seated under a tree, and a cow
feeding ; rev. inscription in Dutch.   Size, 18

614 JEWISH RELIGIOUS MEDALET. Obv. three flower-pots containing flowers; in ex. "Wolden deinder fiend au seinen kin
dern erleht"; rev. inscription in Dutch on two leaves or
tables. Fine ; rare.   Size, 17

615 IVAN WENCESLAUS, of Lichtenstein. Bust; rev. trophy of
arms; in ex. "M. Theresia Aug. Restitutor; rei armamen-
tabiae, 1773." Proof.   Size, 16

616 MEDALET OF MAX. JOSEPH OF BAVARIA. Head ; rev. inscription. Proof.   Size, 14

617 ——— 1842. Obv. inscription; rev. HÖHE DER ELBE
BEI DRESDEN 10 ELL. 16 Z. UEBRO. Fine proof.
                                                       Size, 14

618 ——— Obv. boar, "Ward Ich Versathen;" rev. four I's crowned
forming a cross, "Ten Durch Die Duca." Rare. Size, 14

619 FREDERICK AUGUSTUS, KING OF POLAND. King on horse-
back; rev. throne. Fred. Christian. Obv. angel. "Spei
Publicæ ; rev. inscription ; and one of Charles, Duke of
Wurtenburg—bust ; rev. arms. Size, 14.   3 pieces

620 NATIVITY MEDALET OF LEOPOLD OF AUSTRIA. Obv. inscription ; rev. sun beneath a dove, and inscription. Fine.
                                                       Size, 16

621 FINE LOT OF OLD GERMAN PENNIES, etc., including one of
Albert Margrave of Brandenburg and Duke of Prussia,
1535. A bracteate, etc. Fine and rare lot.   11 pieces

622 THALER OF BAVARIA. Arms of Bavaria and motto of France.
Two-third crown of Leopold I. of Germany, double-headed
eagle ; rev. coat of arms, 1700. Poor.   2 pieces

623 ASSORTED COINS OF HANOVER, Haldenstein, and Germany
generally. Good lot.   19 pieces

624 SELECTED LOT of small coins and groats of the Teutonic Order—Mecklenburg and Salzburg. Rare and valuable lot.
                                                       7 pieces

625 MEDAL JETON. Obv. busts of Alex. of Russia, Francis I. of
Austria, and Fred. William III. of Prussia ; rev. entering of
the allies into Paris; in ex. DEN 31 MÆRZ 1814. Fine.
                                                       Size, 24

626 ——— Female reclining with babe in her arms, another at her
knee, "O Gieb mir Brod Mich Hungert ;" rev. scales, etc.;
in ex. 1816 U 1817. Fine.   Size, 21

627 TURKISH SILVER COINS of Mahmond II., 1808–1839; year of
the hegira, 1223–1255; struck at Constantinople. Very
good, two pierced; rare. Size, 21. 4 pieces

628 —— Others. 3 pieces

629 HINDOSTAN. Rupee of Madras, dated A. H. 1772 (A. D.
1758). Half-rupee, plain edge. Fine. 2 pieces

630 —— Half-rupee and one-eighth rupee, reeded edge. Uncirculated. 2 pieces

---

France, Italy, and Switzerland.

631 PHILIP IV., 1285 (Le Bel) Penny. Short cross in centre,
PHILLIPPVS REX in inner circle, motto in outer circle;
rev. castle in center, fleur-de-lis in circles around. Fine;
rare.

632 CHARLES VI. 1380 (Well-beloved). Grand-blanc. Obv.
KAROLVS FRANCORV REX, spade-shaped shield with
three fleur-de-lis; rev. motto, "Sit Nomen Domini Bene-
dict," cross, fleur-de-lis and crowns in angles. Very fine; rare.

633 HENRY II., 1546. Douzaine (groat-size). Obv. H. crowned
and lilies; rev. cross and lilies.

634 HENRY IV. 1589. Douzaine. Obv. same as last; rev.
cross with lilies and crowns in angles, counterstamped with
a lily; and one of Charles (?). 3 pieces

635 LOUIS XVIII. 1815. Five-francs. Bust; rev. arms crowned.
Ordinary.

636 LOUIS PHILIPPE. 1830. Five-francs. Ordinary.

637 REPUBLIC OF 1848. Five-francs by *Dupré*, 1849; rev. three
figures standing, "Liberté, Egalité, Fraternité." Uncirculated.

638 MEDAL OF NAPOLEON I. Obv. laureated head; rev. two
figures upholding the Emperor on a platform, "Le Senat et
le Peuple." By *Andrieu*. Fine; scratched on cheek.
Size, 26

639 LOUIS XVIII. Bare bust, view of part of the Seine and
Paris; in ex. "Chambre de Commerce du Dept. de la Ch"
Inf"." By *Trolier*. Nearly proof. Size 21

640 GAUL SUBALPINE. Five-francs. Fine.

641 MEDALETS OF C. FERDINAND and Carolina, Duke and
Duchess De Berry. Bastile, and five soldi of Napoleon.
Size, 10. 3 pieces

642 SWITZERLAND. Half-franc, 1851; five-batz, 1873. 2 pieces

Spain, Mexico, **South** and Central America.

643 FERDINAND VII. Proclamation piece of the city of Popayan, bust to r. "Tibi Fides et Amor;" rev. view of the city. "Proclamatus in Civit Popaianensi." Ordinary; rare.

644 BARCELONA. One-peseta. Obv. inscription; rev. lozenge-shaped shield, 1812 and 1813. Poor. 2 pieces

645 CHARLES IV. Shilling, 1801. Counterstamped. Poor.

646 PLATE HALF-DOLLAR of Mexico. Obv. small eagle on a cactus, crowned; rev. "Inauguracion de Agustin Primer Imperador de Mexico, Julio 21 de 1822." Pierced, fine; rare.

647 DOLLAR OF AUGUSTUS (Iturbide). 1823. Bust; rev. eagle on cactus, "Mex., Imperator, Constitut., 8 R, 1 M." Uncirculated; scarce.

648 DOLLAR OF THE REPUBLIC. 1824. Libertad; rev. straight-neck eagle tearing a serpent. Uncirculated.

649 LIBERTAD DOLLAR. 1862. Same as last; uncirculated.

650 REALS OF ITURBIDE and Libertad. 1855. Uncirculated.
2 pieces

651 LIBERTAD DOLLAR OF PERU. 1829. Goddess of Liberty with staff and shield; rev. arms of the Republic on a shield, above, an oak wreath, to r. and l. laurel and palm. Uncirculated; scarce.

652 —— Another. 1831. From a different die, milled edge. Uncirculated.

653 HALF-DOLLAR. 1859. Seated figure of Liberty. Uncirculated.

654 NEW GRANADA. 1848. Arms; rev. BOGOTA, "Dos Reales." Fine.

655 BOLIVIA HALF-DOLLAR. Laureated bust of Bolivar; rev. two llamas lying under a palm-tree, above, nine stars. Uncirculated; rare.

656 QUARTER-REALS OF MEXICO. Leon and Castile. Fine lot; two joined together as cuff buttons. 10 pieces

657 HAYTI 25c., 12c., and 6c. of Boyer and Petion. Obv. bust; rev. martial implements and tree. Uncirculated. 8 pieces

---

Early English Coins.

658 HENRY II. 1154. Penny. Full-face, with sceptre; rev. cross. Fine.

659 HENRY III. 1216. Penny. Full-face; rev. long cross. Fine.

660 EDWARD I. 1272. Head, full-face, crowned, EDWRANGLDN SHVIE; rev. long cross. Scarce.

661 EDWARD II. 1307. Head, full-face, crowned; rev. CIVITAS LONDON. Fine.

662 EDWARD III. 1327. Head; rev. CIVITAS LONDON.
  Fine.

663 —— Another. Poor.

664 —— Half-groat, London. Fine.

665 HENRY V. 1413. Groat. Obv. full-face, crowned; rev.
  VILLA CALISIE. Very fine; rare.

666 EDWARD IV. 1461. Groat. Same; rev. VILLA LON-
  DON. Very fine.

667 HENRY VII. 1485. Groat. Same. Very fine; scarce.

668 —— Equally fine and scarce.

669 HENRY VIII. 1509. Groat. Head, three-quarter face, rev.
  coat of arms. Fair.

670 —— Groat, struck for Ireland. Obv. coat of arms crowned,
  rev. harp crowned. Fine silver. Rare.

671 —— Penny. Obv. full-face crowned; rev. coat of arms.
  Scarce.

672 EDWARD VI. 1547. Sixpence. Bust, full-face, crowned,
  rose to r., VI to l. Fine; pierced.

673 ELIZABETH. 1558. Shilling. MM Sun. Very fine; rare.

674 —— Another. MM Woolsack. Equally fine and rare.

675 —— Sixpence. Very fine, MM Arrow. Scarce.

676 —— Struck for Ireland; rev. harp crowned; on either side E
  and R crowned. Base; fine.

677 —— London twopence. Fair.

——

After the Union.

678 JAMES I. 1602. Shilling, without date. MM fleur-de-lis.
  Good; scarce.

679 —— Another. MM crown. Fine: scarce.

680 CHARLES I. 1625. Half-crown. Obv. king on horseback
  with drawn sword, the Welsh plumes on the horse's head and
  trapping. MM fleur-de-lis. Fine; rare.

681 —— Another. Obv. similar, without plumes. MM Bell.
  Fair; rare.

682 —— Shilling. Head to r., MM flitch; another, head to l., MM
  triangle. Fine. 2 pieces

683 —— Others, MMs crown and harp. Very good. 2 pieces

684 —— Broad shilling, head to l.; rev. coat of arms crowned, on
  either side C and R crowned. Good; scarce.

685 CHARLES II. 1660. Threepence and penny. Good. Threepence pierced. 2 pieces

686 —— Obv. bust, CAR. DG., etc.; rev. two C's crowned,
  FIDE DEFENSOR. Very fine.

687 CHARLES II. Shilling. Obv. bust, laureated head; rev. four
shields arranged in the form **of** a cross, two C's interlinked
crowned, in the angles. Fine; scarce.

688 —— Medal. Bust, head crowned, hair in long curls, VIVAT
CAROLVS REX ; rev. same; loop at either end. Fine.

689 ANNE. 1702. Half-crown. Bust, E beneath; rev. four
shields arranged in the form of a cross. Very good.

690 —— Sixpence. Similar. Fine.

691 —— Medal. Richly draped bust, head laureated; rev. the
queen in armor, holding an olive branch. Ships in offing.
COMPOSITIS, etc. gilt.   Size, 22

692 GEORGE I. 1714. Shilling. Obv. laureated head ; rev. cross
formed by four shields. Fair.

693 —— Medalet. Head laureated ; rev. arms surrounded by
garter, supported by lion and unicorn. Very fine. Size, 18

694 GEORGE II. 1739. Crown. Bust in armor, head laureated ;
rev. four shields arranged in the form of a cross, four roses
in angles. Fine.

695 GEORGE III. 1760. Obv. laureated head ; rev. St. George
slaying the dragon ; on the edge, "Decus et Tutamen. Anno
Regni LX," 1820. By Pistrucci. Uncirculated; rare.

696 —— Bank of Ireland Token. Six shillings. 1804. Fair.

697 —— Bank Token. Three shillings. 1811 and 1813. Good.
       2 pieces

698 —— "XXX Pence Irish." 1808. Good.

699 —— "1s. 6d." 1811. Fine.

700 —— Medal. Laureated head ; rev. shield held by two savages. "Free trade to Africa," etc. 1750. Fine proof.

701 —— Maundy Money, 4d. 3d. 2d. and 1d. Proof. 4 pieces

702 GEORGE IV. 1820. Half-crown, 1826. Fair.

703 WILLIAM IV. 1830. Half-crown, 1836. Almost uncirculated.

704 —— One Rupee. 1835. Fair.

705 VICTORIA. 1837. Rupees of 1840 and 1862. Uncirculated.
       2 pieces

706 —— Model Pennies, copper.   2 pieces

APPENDIX.

United States Cents.

707 1793. Wreath, "One hundred for a dollar" on the edge.
Date a little weak, otherwise very good; rare.

708 1794. Very little circulated Cent, but shows the signs of cor-
rosion. Very desirable; rare.

709 1795. Plain edge, thin planchet; fair.

710 1796. Liberty cap. Fair.

711 ——— Fillet head. Better than last.

712 1797. Fine.

713 1798. Very good.

714 1799. Very fine. Seldom found better; very rare.

715 1800. Two varieties, and 1801-2-3. All fair, and one 1800
good.   4 pieces

716 1804. Broken die. Fine; rare.

717 1805. Very good.

718 1806. Rather better than last. Very good for date; scarce.

719 1807. Fair.

720 1808. Better than fair; scarce.

721 1809. Obverse rather poor; rev. good. Scarce.

722 1810. Fair; scarce.

723 1811. Fine and sharp; slightly corroded. Scarce.

724 1812. Equally fine; scarce.

725 1813. Very good; scarce.

726 1814. Two varieties; ordinary.   2 pieces

727 1816. Poor. Two varieties of 1817; poor.   3 pieces

728 1818. Fine.

729 1819–20–21. Poor.   3 pieces

730 1822. Good. 1823–24–25. Ordinary; scarce.   4 pieces

731 1826. Fine.

732 1827–28–29. Ordinary.   3 pieces

733 1830. Very good.

734 1831. Ordinary.

735 1832. Very fine.

736 1833–34–35–36–37–38. Fair to ordinary.   6 pieces

737 1839. "Booby head." Fair.

48 Appendix.

1 738 1840. Ordinary.
739 1841. Very fine.
740 1846 to 1857. inclusive. All fair.   10 pieces

Half-Cents.

741 1793. Fine; rare.
742 1794. Very good; rare.
743 1795. Thin planchet. Rather better; rare.
744 1800–04–05–06–07–08–09. Fair to good.   7 pieces
745 1825–26–28–29–32–34–35–49–50–51–53–55–56–57. All fine.
                                                  14 pieces

Colonials.

746 1786. "Venuontensium Res. Publica," seven trees;
       "Quarta Decima Stella." Fine; rare.
747 1786. "Auctori Vermon." baby head; "Inde et Lib." Un-
       usually fine, and in this condition rare.
748 1787. "Vermon Auctori;" rev. Britannia. Nearly uncircula-
       ted, but very considerably corroded on the obv.; rare.
749 1787. New York Cent. Obv. "Immunis Columbia," fig-
       ure of Liberty seated; rev. "E. Pluribus Unum," eagle.
       Rarely found as fine, and in this condition very rare.
750 1788. Massachusetts Cent. Obv. eagle, "Massachusetts;"
       rev. "Commonwealth," Indian standing. Almost uncircu-
       lated; rare.
751 1787. New York Cent. "Nova Eborac," head to r.; rev.
       "Inde et Lib." Fine; rare.
752 1787. Conn. Cent. "Auctori Connec," head to l.; rev.
       "Inde et Lib." Very little circulated, a little rusty on obv.;
       rev. fine; desirable.
753 1788. Auctori Connec. Head to r. Good.
754 1787–88. Varieties; all fair.   4 pieces
755 1786. New Jersey Cent. Fine.
756 1787. Another, different type. Very fine.
757 1786–87. Varieties. Fair to fine.   3 pieces
758 1783. "Nova Constelatio." U. S. type. Fine.
758* —— Others, script type. Fair and poor.   2 pieces
759 1722. Rosa Americana Penny. Rose without a crown. Fair.
760 —— Another. Poor; pierced.
760* 1773. Virginia Cent. Fair.

British Copper Coins.

Scotch.

761 James VI. (?) Small copper coin. Obv. thistle; rev. lion.
       Poor; rare.

762 CHARLES II. 1660. Obv. C.R." beneath a crown ; rev. this-
30   tle. Fair ; rare.
763 WILLIAM AND MARY. 1668. Obv. monogram beneath a
   crown ; rev. thistle. Good ; rare.

Irish.

764 ELIZABETH. 1558. Farthing. Obv. arms ; rev. harp. Fine ;
   very rare.
765 —— Another. Fair.
766 CHARLES I. 1625. Obv. two sceptres crossed, crown in centre ; rev. harp. Very fine ; rare.
767 CHARLES II. 1660. Half-penny. Obv. bust ; rev. harp.
   Poor.
768 JAMES II. 1685. Half-pennies. "Hibernia." Varieties.
   3 pieces
769 —— Others. Poor.   3 pieces
770 WILLIAM AND MARY. 1688. Half-penny. Obv. their busts
   jugata. Good ; scarce.
771 GEORGE III. 1760. Voce Populi. Varieties ; poor. 4 pieces.
772 JAMES II. Gun Money. Jan., 1689. XII. Fine.
773 —— May, 1689. XXX. Uncirculated
774 —— July VI. and Aug. XXX. and XII. Fine.   4 pieces
775 —— Oct., 1689. XXX. and XII. Very good.
776 —— July, 1689, VI. and Oct., 1689, XXX. Fair.
777 —— May, 1690, XXX. and June, 1690, XII. Good.
778 —— Crown, 1690. The king on horseback ; rev. arms arranged in the form of a cross. Uncirculated.
779 —— Others. One fine.   2 pieces

English.

780 CHARLES II. 1660. Obv. bust. CAROLUS A CAROLO.
   Half-penny and farthing. The farthing fine ; rare. 2 pieces
781 MARY II. 1688. Pattern Farthing. Obv. bust ; rev. rose.
   EX CANDORE DECVS. Fine ; rare.
782 ANNA. 1703. Farthing Token. Obv. bust ; rev. arms on
   four shields arranged in the form of a cross. Often mistaken
   for the copper farthing. Two varieties ; rare. Brass. 2 pcs
783 GEO. I. 1714. Half-penny and Farthing. Fine. 2 pieces
784 GEO. II. 1729. Half-penny. Uncirculated.
785 —— Farthings. Three varieties ; good lot.   3 pieces
786 GEO. III. 1760. Two-pence. Letters incused ; uncirculated.
787 —— Penny. Same type. Proof ; rare.
788 —— Pattern Farthing, 1782. Obv. laureated head, flowing
   hair ; rev. arms. Lettered edge, ornamental rim. Uncirculated ; *rare.*

789 Geo. III. Farthings, 1773 and 1799. Varieties; one uncirculated, the other fine. 2 pieces

790 ——— Half-pennies. Varieties; fine. 2 pieces

791 ——— Isle of Man Penny. Rev. trinacria. Fine.

792 ——— Isle of Man Half-penny. Rev. trinacria. Fine.

793 Pennies, Half-pennies, Farthings, and Half-farthings of Geo. I., II., III., and IV., William IV and Victoria. Fine lot ; no duplicates. 18 pieces

794 Tradesmen's Half-penny Tokens. Fine proof impressions, Petersfield, Lancaster, and a medalet of Geo. IV as Prince Regent. 3 pieces

795 ——— Others, uncirculated. Fine lot. 5 pieces

796 ——— Others. All fine ; desirable lot ; no duplicates. 18 pieces

797 North Wales. Penny and half-penny ; Druid's head. Very fine. 2 pieces

798 South Wales. Dundee and Spence farthings. Fine and rare lot. 4 pieces

799 Penny Size. Holloway's card ; Jersey ; Nova Scotia, etc. Fine lot. 5 pieces

800 Canadian Half-penny Tokens. Good lot ; no duplicates. 20 pieces

801 East India Company. Coppers of various sizes, etc. 30 pieces

Miscellaneous.

802 Medals and Jetons of the 16th and 17th Centuries. The former, thin pieces with elaborated and finely executed coats of arms and armorial devices, once much used in France and Germany as coins ; they were principally struck by the nobility. The Jetons were political, and are broader. Fine and valuable lot. No duplicates. 9 pieces

803 ——— Similar. No duplicates. As good as last. 10 pieces

804 ——— Principally Jetons. Fine. 10 pieces

805 ——— Fine lot. 10 pieces

There are only two or three duplicates in the whole 39 pices.

806 French Copper Coins of Louis XVI., Louis Philippe, Chas. X., and the two Republics. All large ; good lot. 12 pieces

807 ——— Henry III., Louis XIII. and XV., Nap. I. and II., and two Republics. Small. 30 pieces

808 Germany, Italy, Turkey, Papal States, etc. Good lot. 50 pieces

809 Similar Lot. 130 pieces

810 Brunswick and Luneberg. Wild Man Pennies ; different dates and varieties. 16 pieces

811 SELECTED LOT of small German Coins, mostly uncirculated
2   and fine. Card of the Hotel de Toelas, Alkamnar, C.
    Kowats, Hannu, " Gut fur einen bier," etc.   No duplicates.
                                                        30 pieces
813 MEDALETS IN BRASS. Nap. III., Princess Clotilde, etc., with
1   loops.   9 pieces
814 A CLASSIFIED SERIES of Coins of the sequestrated cities of
11 Germany. Each city in a separate envelope, with descrip-
    tion. Including Arnheim, Augsburg, Batemburg, Einbeck,
    Erfurt, Eichstadt, Emden, Frisia, Halle, Halberstadt, Hanim,
    Heidelberg, Hasselt, Hildesheim, Huissen, Hutchen, Karls-
    ruhe, Leige, Limburg, Lindau, Mansfeld, Marsberg, Minden,
    Mirzburg, Walterhausen, Warendorf, Wurtemburg, Regens-
    burg, Reckheim, Utrecht, Saalfeld, Saha, Settin, Stevens-
    worth, Straulsund. Stozburg, Zeulsnroda, and Zeeland.
    Comprising many rare coins, tokens, klippes, etc. A valu-
    able collection and not easily duplicated.   182 pieces
815 UNCLASSIFIED GERMAN COINS from the Stenz Collection, in
    fine condition. Some rare. There is an almost complete
    series of Pfenning and **Hellers** from 1700 to 1870. Desir-
    able lot.   315 pieces
816 AMERICAN SHINPLASTERS, cards, political tokens, Washington
3   medalets, etc., in copper and brass.   30 pieces

Copper Medals.

817 CATHERINE II. OF RUSSIA. 1762. Obv. her bust in annor;
    on her head the helmet of Pallas surmounted by an owl;
5   rev. Empress seated; before her, Mars supporting a kneel-
    ing figure who presents her a crown and sceptre on a cush-
    ion; near them an angel pointing upward at a figure seated
    on a cloud. A splendid medal, by *Waechter*. Rare.
                                                        Size, 42
818 —— 1763. Obv. bust; rev. two females. Fine.   Size, 32
819 MEDAL TO COMMEMORATE the opening of the railway between
    Paris and Brussels. Thick medal, figures in high relief. By
    Hart. Nickel-plated. Fine.   Size, 46
820 ALEXANDER I. OF RUSSIA. Obv. bare bust; rev. view of the
    Winter Palace, 1839; on the margin, the signs of the Zodiac.
    Nearly proof. By *Gure*.   Size, 41
821 COMMEMORATIVE MEDAL. 1819. Obv. three giant figures
    clad in lion skins trampling on their fallen foes, AUX
    BRAVES ARMEES FRANCAISES; rev. inscription in
    ten lines. Very fine. By *J. P. Droz*.   Size, 33
822 MORTUARY MEDAL. Obv. bare bust of Carl Ferdinand; rev.
    angel embracing an urn which surmounts a tombstone.
    FLEBILIS OCCIDIT FER. XIV. MDCCXX.; in ex. SO-
    CIETAS ARTIBVS AMICA PATRONO. Fine. By *Gay-
    rard*.   Size, 32

823 CHARLES I. OF ENGLAND. Obv. bust in armour, head bare
50   rev. view of a bleak country; above, a hand issuing from the
        clouds holding a crown, VIRTVT. EX. ME. FORTVNAM.
        EX. ALIIS. Proof; rare.   Size, 30

824 MILITARY MEDAL OF ROUSSEAU. Obv. his figure in a Roman
        toga; seated; rev. NE A GENEVE, MORT A PARIS
        NONVILLE, EN MDCCLXXVII, and inscription in seven
        lines. Very rare. By Bory.   Size, 42

825 NAPOLEON I. Obv. laureated head, "Napoleon King et Roi;"
        rev. two helmeted female heads, on one a galley—Paris—on
        the other, the she-wolf and twins—Rome. Fine proof. By
        Andrieu.   Size, 25

826 —— Obv. laureated head; rev. interior of the Musée Napo-
        leon. By Andrieu. Proof.   Size, 22

827 COMMEMORATIVE MEDAL. Obv. head of Louis XVIII. FI-
        DELITE DEVOUEMENT; rev. a crown and fleur-de-lis;
        beneath, a five-pointed star bearing a circular shield, on it,
        in the centre a fleur-de-lis. By Andrieu. Fine. Size, 26

828 —— Obv. head of Louis XVIII.; rev. France and America
..0   personified leaning against a column, surmounted by a bust
        of Mercury; GALLIA ET AMERICA FOEDERATA;
        in ex. NOVIS COMMERCIORVM PACTIS IVNCTAE.
        By Andrieu. Fine.   Size, 32

829 BASTILE MEDAL. Obv. PRISE DE LA BASTILE; in ex.
        14 JUILLET, 1789; rev. view of the "Donjon" at Vin-
        cennes. By Regel. Proof.   Size, 27

830 J. I. GUILLOTIN. Obv. bust; rev. inscription in nine lines.
        Proof.   Size, 18
        This medal was struck in honor of the inventor of the guillotine and
        is rare.

831 NAPOLEON III. Election medal; bust; rev. inscription; obv.
        laureated heads of Louis XIV. and Louis Philippe; rev.
        "Chateau" at Versailles; obv. heads of Albert and Victoria;
        rev. Nap. III. and Eugenie. Fine. Size, 16.   3 pieces

832 FREDERICK II. (The Great) of Prussia. Obv. bust; rev.
        eagle, COELITUS; rev. battle of Rosbach. Fine.   2 pieces

833 COMMEMORATIVE MEDALS of Christopher Columbus and
        Christopher Hussland. Fine. Size, 26.   2 pieces

834 GREGORY XVI. and Pius IX. Fine. Size, 27.   2 pieces

835 QUAINT OLD MEDAL of Pope Innocent X.; cast: contempo-
        rary; Pope Julius II., and others. Fine lot. Size, 23.
                                                         4 pieces

836 REFORMATION MEDAL. 1539. Obv. bust of Joachim II. of
        Brandenburg, with sceptre and sword; rev. sacrament. Rare.
                                                         Size, 23

837 COMMEMORATIVE MEDAL of the third centennial of the Refor-
        mation at Geneva; rev. open Bible. Fine.   Size, 21

837* FERDINAND, Duke of Wirtemburg. Obv. bust; rev. inscription. Fine proof. Size, 21

838 MORTUARY MEDAL. Obv. bust of Charles Ferdinand ; rev. inscription in eight lines within a triple oak wreath. Beautiful medal, by *Pfeuffer*. Size, 38

839 WASHINGTON Cabinet. U. S. mint. Fine proof. By *Pacquet*. Size, 38

840 COL. JOHN EGAR HOWARD. For intrepidity at the battle of Cowpens. Fine. By *Duvivier*. Size, 30

841 COL. WILLIAM WASHINGTON. In honor of same battle. Proof. By *Duvivier*. Size, 30

842 CAPT. STEPHEN DECATUR. For the Capture of the Frigate Macedonian, Oct. 25, 1812. Proof by *Furst*. Size, 40

843 CAPT. OLIVER HOWARD PERRY. In honor of the Victory on Lake Erie. Jan. 31, 1814. Proof by *Furst*. Size, 36

844 COM. EDWARD PREBLE. In honor of the victory at Tripoli, 1804. Fine ; *rare*. Size, 40

845 MAJ.-GEN. WINFIELD SCOTT. For distinguished services in the battle of Chapultepec, Vera Cruz, Cerro Gordo, etc. By Congress. By *C. C. Wright*. Fine proof. Size, 56

846 MAJ.-GEN. ZACHARY TAYLOR. For victory at Buena Vista, Feb. 23, 1847. Splendid proof. by *Wright*. Size, 56

847 FRANKLIN MEDAL ; rev. "Erepuit Cœlo," etc. Fine proof. by *Dupre*. Size, 29

848 BRIG SOMERS. For the rescue of her officers and men in the harbor of Vera Cruz, Dec. 10, 1846. By *Wright*. Fine proof. Size, 36

849 BUST OF GEO. II. ; rev. William Penn in the act of offering the pipe of peace to an Indian. 1757. "Let us look to the most high," etc. Broken dies. Proof. Size, 28

850 KITTANNING DESTROYED by COL. ARMSTRONG, Sept. 8, 1756. From broken dies. Proof. Size, 28

851 WASHINGTON ALLSTON. By the Art Union, 1847. By C. C. Wright. Very fine. Size, 40

852 IGNATIUS LOYOLA. Founder of the Order of Sons of Jesus. Obv. bust with cap on his head, and an open book in his hand. S.IGN.DE.LOY.S.I.F. ; rev. the saint asleep on the shore, guarded by angels ; a ship in offing. Fine old metal uni *very rare*. Size, 22

853 HENRY IV. OF FRANCE. Obv. his bust ; rev. bust, MARGA-RITA, AVSTRIA. Cast, with an ornamental rim like a snake's body, raised. Curious old medal. Size, 26

854 BAPTISMAL MEDAL. Obv. St. John baptizing Christ ; rev. inscription ; and another. Size, 21. 2 pieces

855 MONS-RONS, CINQ-SOLS, DEUX Sols ; Leopold, King of Belgium, and others. Fine lot. Size, 21. 7 pieces

856 HEAD OF CHRIST ; rev. "Love ye each other ;" "Souvenir," Leopold of Belgium, and others. Average size, 18. 5 pieces

857 MARTIN LUTHER. Jun. To commemorate the completion
of a Lutheran church in Amsterdam, 1826. Fine and rare.
Size, 19

858 LA FAYETTE. Obv. Military bust; rev. " Il a commandé la
Garde Nationale Parisienne en 1789, 1790, et 1791." Proof.
By *Dumarest*. Size, 22

859 PRINCE ALBERT. Pres. of the Royal Crown. In commemo-
ration of the extinction of slavery. Charles Gray, Member
of Parliament, " House of Temperance," and others. Fine
lot. Some proof. Av. size, 28. 9 pieces

---

860 NEW YORK AND LONDON CRYSTAL PALACE MEDALS. *White
Metal.* Size, 31. 3 pieces

861 HENRY CLAY, Abraham Lincoln, and Thos. Swann, Mayor of
Baltimore. *W.M.* Size, 28. 3 pieces

862 CRYSTAL PALACE. Ludwig I. of Bavaria, German Jubilee
Medal, and others. *W.M.* Size, 24. 7 pieces

863 STONEWALL JACKSON, Frederick Magnus. Fine. *W.M.* Size,
38. 2 pieces

864 MEDAL TO COMMEMORATE THE NAVAL BATTLE IN VIGO BAY,
1702. Obv. view of the battle; rev. trophy of arms, etc.,
upheld by a lion, unicorn, and eagle. Fine; rare. *Lead.*
Size, 36.

Never before described in an American catalogue.

Miscellaneous.

865 SIBERIA. Large copper coin, struck by Catherine II. Obv.
cipher of her name; rev. two foxes upholding a shield.
Rare. Size, 24

866 SIERRA LEONE COMPANY. One cent, 1791. Proof.

867 FIVE KOPECS OF RUSSIA and One Daler of Sweden. 2 pieces

868 COINS OF THE ISLAND OF SUMATRA. Rooster. Varieties.
3 pieces

869 TURKISH and East Indian Coins. 15 pieces

870 CENTRAL AND SOUTH AMERICAN Coins, with a few Canadian,
etc. 20 pieces

871 UNCLASSIFIED *Silver Coins* of the sequestrated German cities,
with a few others; all more or less base; from the Stone
Collection. Many important ones are represented; none
of them are illegible, and quite a collection can be made out
of the lot. 50 pieces

872 —— Similar lot. 50 pieces

873 —— Same. 100 pieces

872 BARBADOES half-penny. Obv. crowned head of a negro, " I
serve ; " rev. Neptune in his car, drawn through the waves.
Very fine ; rare.

5c

Cameos and Intaglios.

873 CAMEO HEAD OF AUGUSTUS on agate-onyx, light-brown on
dark slate-colored tablet. Very fine specimen of the quatre-
cento. 1⅓ x ⅞ in.

874 —— of a blackamoor. Chocolate on white ground, same pe-
riod. *Very fine.* Size ⅞ in.

875 —— of a female. ⅓ face, pink on chalcedony ground. Very
fine and suitable for a lady's ring. ⅜ in.

876 —— of a warrior in helmet, on a beautiful dark carnelian. A
gem. ⅓ in. sq.

877 —— of a female. White on chalcedony. Fine. ⅜ in.

878 —— of a female, draped, on a sardonyx of five layers ; the
head on one of the white layers, the other three in the table.
Very fine ring-stone. ⅜ in.

879 MATCHED PAIR OF CAMEO HEADS. Suitable for buttons.
17th century. ⅞ in. 2 pieces

880 —— Another. ⅞ in. 2 pieces

881 —— Same. Male and female heads. ⅞ in. 2 pieces

882 —— Others. Heads of two Popes or priests on onyx. ⅛ in.
2 pieces,

7⸲883 SMALL CAMEOS. Female heads. Very good. ⅞ in.
3 pieces

884 MATCHED PAIR OF INTAGLIO HEADS. Shakespeare and a hel-
meted head. Will make a beautiful pair of buttons. ⅛ in.
2 pieces

885 SMALL BLOOD-STONE, suitable for a ring. The device is a
thistle, surrounding it is the motto of the MacGregors of
Scotland, " Wha dare meddle wi' me ? " Very fine. ⅛ in.

ANOTHER PROPERTY.

Cut Stones, Jewelry, and Gems.

(The following lots were catalogued from the owner's MSS.)

886 LARGE, ROUND RED AGATE CUP, suitable for a receptacle for
gems, jewelry, etc. Very fine and valuable. 6¼ in. in diameter.

887 —— Another. Equally as fine ; same size.

888 LARGE, RED AGATE CUP. Oval. Very fine. 5½ in. in diameter.

889 ORIENTAL ONYX CUP. Round. As fine as last.

890 LAPIS LAZULI CUP. Oval, with pedestal. Height, 5½ in diameter, 3¼ in.

891 ROCK-CRYSTAL CROSS. Very fine and valuable. 4½ in. high.

892 —— Another. 3¾ in.

893 SIBERIAN MALACHITE CROSS. Fine. 1½ in.

894 ONYX CROSS. Small; fine. 2¼ in.

895 CARNELIAN CROSS. Fine. 2⅝ in.

896 LARGE MOSAIC JEWELRY CASE. Inlaid with precious stones of all kinds. Mounted in fire-gilt frame; the bottom being one large agate. *Very fine.* 5 x 3 in.

897 ONE PAIR BUTTONS. Engraved with animals. Black onyx. 2 pieces

898 ONYX PIN. Engraved with head of the Empress Eugenie. Fine.

899 BLOODSTONE INTAGLIO. Representing an eagle. Engraved with acid. Fine.

900 —— Flower.

901 —— Duplicate.

The ten following lots are oval, red and black Oriental agate intaglios engraved in Roman style. The subjects are Christ, the Virgin, Evangelists, etc. They are very fine and rare.

902 A PAIR. Selected. 2 pieces

903 —— Another. 2 pieces

904 —— Another. 2 pieces

905 —— Another. 2 pieces

906 —— Another. 2 pieces

907 —— Another. 2 pieces

908 TWO PAIRS. Selected. 4 pieces

909 —— Same. 4 pieces

910 —— Repetition of last. 4 pieces

911 THREE more. 3 pieces

912 PAIR CAMEO SLEEVE-BUTTONS. Pink-sardonyx. Flora and companion. Very fine. 2 pieces

913 —— Mignon and companion. 2 pieces

914 MALACHITE ANIMAL HEAD. Roman engraved.

915 —— Repetition of last.

916 —— Another.

917 ANIMAL HEAD ON CORAL. Roman engraving.

918 —— On agate. Same.

919 ONE LARGE AGATE CAMEO. "Fantasia."

920 ONE LARGE ROUND AGATE CUP. Red.   Diam., 4¾ in

921 ONE OVAL AGATE CUP. Engraved. "Souvenir." Diam., 3⅛ in.

922 —— Black and white onyx cup. Engraved. " Amitée." Diam., 3¾ in.

923 —— Round onyx cup, with pedestal. Black inside and gray outside. Fine ; very rare.   Diam., 3½, height, 3⅛ in.

924 TWO OVAL LAPIS LAZULI CUPS with pedestals. Height and diam., 3⅞ in., 2 pieces

925 ONE ONYX CROSS. Fine.   Length, 2¾ in.

926 AGATE CROSS. Fine.   Length, 2½ in.

927 LARGE MOSAIC JEWELRY CASE. Inlaid with precious stones. Very fine and rare.   4¼ x 2¾ in.

928 ONYX SLEEVE-BUTTONS. Black and white. A pair.   2 pieces

929 —— Similar.   2 pieces

930 —— Duplicate.   2 pieces

931 AGATE SEAL. Mounted in fine silver.

932 —— Another.

933 —— Duplicate.

934 —— Same.

935 —— Repetition.

936 —— A pair.   2 pieces

937 AGATE PENHOLDER. Mounted in fine silver.

938 —— Another.

939 —— Same.

940 RED SARDONYX CAMEO. "Virginia." Round.

941 —— Mercury. Similar.

942 ROCK-CRYSTAL SEAL. Very fine.

943 —— Others.   2 pieces

944 —— Similar.   2 pieces

945 —— Another large.

946 —— Repetition of last.

947 ROCK CRYSTAL SMELLING-BOTTLE. Very fine.

948 —— Another. Different shape.

949 —— Another.

950 ONE DOZEN red agate knife-handles.   12 pieces

951 HALF-DOZEN onyx agate knife-handles.   6 pieces

952 PAIR AMETHYST pendeloques.   2 pieces

953 SEAL. Rock-crystal. Large.

954 —— Another.

955 —— Agate and onyx.   2 pieces

956 —— Others.   2 pieces

957 —— Another.

958 Seal. Others. Larger. 2 pieces
959 —— Agate. 2 pieces
960 —— Similar. 2 pieces
961 —— Same. 3 pieces
962 — — Very large. Length, 4 in.
963 —— Repetition. Length, 4 in.
964 —— Similar. Length, 4 in.
965 —— Onyx. Very rare. Length, 5½ in.
966 —— Duplicate. Length, 5¾ in.
967 Triangular Charms. Topaz. 5 pieces
968 —— Similar. 5 pieces
969 —— Others. 5 pieces
970 —— Duplicates. 10 pieces
971 —— Lapis Lazuli.
972 —— Same.
973 —— Bloodstone. Large. 2 pieces
974 —— Same. Small. 3 pieces
975 —— Topaz. Hebrew engraving. Fine.

976 to 984 Roman Rubies. 140 carats. To be sold in nine lots. Eight lots containing 15 carats each, and one lot 20 carats.
985 —— 9 carats (102 pieces). Extra fine.
986 —— 31 carats. Large.
987 —— 22 carats (2 pieces).
988 Mexican Opals. 14½ carats. 4 pieces
989 Pearls. One fine pearl, 121 grains.
990 —— 50 grains. 23 pieces
991 —— 77 grains. 20 pieces
992 —— 79 grains. 25 pieces
993 —— 32 grains. Oriental; large. 7 pieces
994 —— 37 grains. Oriental; large. 8 pieces
995 —— 43 grains. Oriental; large. 8 pieces
996 —— 49 grains. Oriental; large. 8 pieces
997 —— One fine pearl, 26 grains. Oriental; large.
998 Pink Topaz. Fine; cut. 4 carats.
999 Oriental Sapphire. Cut. 5 carats.
1000 —— 2 carats.
1001 One piece of Diamond Carbon. 1½ carats.
1002 —— Same. 1½ carats.
1003 —— Same. 3 carats.
1004 Sapphire. 29 carats, white, rough. One piece.
1005 —— 17 carats, yellow, rough. 9 pieces

1006 SAPPHIRE. 23 carats, yellow, rough.   12 pieces
1007–1009 NECKLACES. Onyx. 50 beads each, 3 lots.   Sold separately.
1010–1012 —— Red Agate. 50 beads each, 3 lots. Sold separately.
1013–1015 —— Bloodstone. 50 " " 3 " " "
1016–1017 —— Rock-Crystal. 50 beads each, 2 lots. Sold separately.
1018–1020 —— Amethyst. 50 beads each, 3 lots. Sold separately.
1021–1023 —— " 100 " " 3 " " "
1024–1025 —— Small Black and White Onyx. 50 beads each.
           2 pieces
1026 SET OF SLEEVE-BUTTONS AND STUDS. Chrysoprase.
1027 OVAL SLEEVE-BUTTONS. Chrysoprase. Pair.   2 pieces
1028 LARGE ROUND ONYX, with one white stripe.
1029 LARGE OVAL ONYX, with one white stripe.
1030–1033 40 AMETHYSTS AND TOPAZ. Cut. In 4 lots, 10 in each lot.
1034 BLOODSTONE Knife-handle.
1035 PETRIFIED WOOD Knife-handle.
1036 MALACHITE Cane Head.
1037 LAPIS LAZULI Cane Head.
1038 SLEEVE-BUTTONS. Lapis Lazuli. Oval.   2 pieces
1039 —— Same.   2 pieces
1040 —— Same, round.   2 pieces
1041 —— Similar.   2 pieces
1042 —— Repetition.   2 pieces
1043 LAPIS LAZULI Ring Stones. Large.   4 pieces
1044 —— Same.   2 pieces
1045 SET OF SLEEVE-BUTTONS AND STUDS. Lapis Lazuli.
1046 SET OF PIN AND BUTTONS. Siberian Malachite.
1047 —— Duplicate.
1048 MALACHITE SCARF-PIN. Mounted.
1049 —— Same.
1050 —— Siberian. Pendants ; pair.   2 pieces
1051 —— Same.   2 pieces
1052 LARGE GREEN MOSS AGATE. 2¼ x 4 inches.
1053 AGATE BUCKLE.
1054 INDIAN NOSE RINGS. Agate.   3 pieces
1055 —— Same.   3 pieces
1056 ONE LARGE PINK AMETHYST.
1057 SET LARGE AMETHYST.   3 pieces
1058 —— Same.   3 pieces

1059 ONE LARGE ROUND ONYX CAMEO STONE.
1060 ONE LARGE OVAL ONYX CAMEO STONE.
1061 TWO LARGE OVAL ONYX CAMEO STONES.   2 pieces
1062 ONE RED ONYX CAMEO STONE.
1063 ONE SET RED ONYX CAMEO STONES.   3 pieces
1064 VERY RARE AND PERFECT ROUND ROCK-CRYSTAL SEAL.
1065 LARGE RED AGATE CANE HEADS.   2 pieces
1066 ONE AGATE CROSS. 2½ inches long.
1067 SEVERAL LOTS of selected Stones for Collections, consisting of Agates, Topaz, etc., etc.

ERRATA.

Line 25 of Introduction, read quality instead of variety.

Lot 301, second line, for goblet read globe.

Lot 487 should be read after lot 490.

Orders for this Sale will be Executed by

JOHN W. HASELTINE, 1225 Chestnut Street, Philadelphia, Pa.

HENRY G. SAMPSON, Cor. Fulton St. and Broadway, N. Y.

EDWARD COGAN, 408 State Street, Brooklyn, N. Y.

HENRY AHLBORN, 33 Exchange Street, Boston.

EDWARD FROSSARD, Irvington, N. Y.

SCOTT & CO., 146 Fulton Street, New York.

DAVID PROSKEY, 194 Washington Street, New York.

S. H. HARZFELD, 1713 Park Avenue, Philadelphia.

T. R. STROBRIDGE, No. 1 Gates Avenue, Brooklyn, N. Y.

Or, by the Auctioneers.

————•+◆+•————

W. H. STROBRIDGE, Antiquary,

No. 1 GATES AVENUE, BROOKLYN.

————•+◆+•————

CORRESPONDENCE SOLICITED.

Collections of Coins, Bric-a-brac, Antiques, etc., bought or Catalogued for sale.

Letters may be addressed to him or to his son, T. R. STROBRIDGE, at the above address.

www.ingramcontent.com/pod-product-compliance
Lightning Source LLC
Chambersburg PA
CBHW021226260626
47172CB00002B/621